THE LAW OF MATT COBURN

Felton looked up at Coburn. "What do I do?" he asked, "I guess it's not enough just to walk down there with a badge."

Coburn waited a moment before he spoke.

"No," he said finally, "it isn't. Not every man can do it—you might be one of them. I'd take a shotgun if I were you. Go down there and tell them the law, and the first one who gives you any back talk, just give him the butt of it in their teeth. If he reaches for a gun . . . shoot him."

THE EMPTY LAND
A Whiplash Action Western
BY LOUIS L'AMOUR

THE EMPTY LAND

LOUIS L'AMOUR

BANTAM BOOKS · TORONTO · NEW YORK

THE EMPTY LAND
A Bantam Book / January 1969
2nd printing .... February 1969   3rd printing ...... October 1969
4th printing .... April 1970
New Bantam edition / April 1971

2nd printing ...... August 1971	9th printing . November 1975
3rd printing ...... January 1972	10th printing .... January 1977
4th printing .. September 1972	11th printing .... May 1977
5th printing .... April 1973	12th printing .... October 1977
6th printing .. September 1973	13th printing .... May 1978
7th printing ...... October 1973	14th printing .... April 1979
8th printing .... August 1974	15th printing .... January 1980

16th printing

ISBN 0-553-13858-8

Published simultaneously in the United States and Canada

Bantam Books are published by Bantam Books, Inc. Its trademark, consisting of the words "Bantam Books" and the por-
trayal of a bantam, is Registered in U.S. Patent and Trademark
Office and in other countries. Marca Registrada. Bantam
Books, Inc., 666 Fifth Avenue, New York, New York 10019.

PRINTED IN THE UNITED STATES OF AMERICA

To My Father . . .
who knew what it meant to wear the badge.

THE EMPTY LAND

CHAPTER 1

In Europe, Pope Gregory the Great had died, in Ireland the Golden Age of scholarship was at its height, and on the Continent the Merovingian kings ruled much of what is now Germany and France.

In Southeast Asia the little kingdom of Champa, now called South Vietnam, was locked in a life-and-death struggle for its independence, with China and what is now North Vietnam.

It was the seventh century, and the great T'ang dynasty was rising in China, while across the Asian continent a relatively unknown young man named Mohammed sat meditating in Mecca, conceiving the religious teachings that were to dominate civilization for the next seven hundred years.

In what was someday to be known as western Utah, a hungry coyote trotted across a barren slope.

The coyote had no awareness of history beyond the memory of where his food had been obtained in the past, nor had he any realization of the sequence of events he was soon to start in motion, a sequence that was to enrich several men and at least one woman, and was to bring sudden and violent death by bullet or blade to at least forty men.

1

All of that lay more than eleven hundred years in the future, but it was the coyote that began it.

The desert slope across which the coyote trotted was no different to the eye from a thousand other such slopes, falling steeply away to a boulder-strewn wash that remained dry except after the infrequent rains, when it might run six to eight feet deep with rushing water, only to dwindle away to nothing in an hour or so.

The slope itself was a litter of sand, broken rock, low-growing brush and an occasional juniper.

There was nothing to draw the attention, even less to hold it. There was only the deep green of the junipers against the sand-colored slope, broken here and there by the broken teeth of exposed ledges or outcroppings.

Over the centuries the slope had remained relatively unchanged. A rock rolled here, a cedar sprang up over yonder, a bush died, a passing animal left droppings. The sun and the wind moved over the slope.

The coyote remembered a chipmunk that lived somewhere near the crest. It was a very wily chipmunk, but the coyote was passing his way and might prove luckier than in the past.

Wise in the ways of coyotes, the chipmunk was alert to his coming and, not averse to a little game of tease and tag, waited until the coyote charged, then flipped his tail and ducked into a hole.

Whining with eagerness, the coyote dug at the hole, scattering sand and gravel behind him. Then his claws scraped on rock, uncovering a narrow crack, much too small for a coyote, but perfect for a chipmunk.

Frustrated and furious, the coyote gnawed at the edges of rock, breaking off a few brittle flakes; after that he trotted around behind, searching for another approach, but there was none.

Finally, after much restless pacing and some useless digging, the coyote gave up, deciding the small bite the chipmunk offered was unworthy of so much effort, and he trotted off, pausing only occasionally for a backward glance.

Two months later, it rained. The earth was still loose where the coyote had dug, and the trickle of water off the outcropping came eagerly upon it, filling the hole, then trickling over the edge and starting a tiny stream that hurried down the slope to join the large waters rushing through the wash. The tiny stream carried along with it a small burden of silt and sand, mingled with some minute fragments from the rock, broken off by the teeth of the coyote. When the flash flood ran itself out, the flakes were dropped and left lying to mingle with the sand.

Over the years rains pounded at the slope, and the wind worried it. A juniper seed fell into the crack in the rock, found some slight nourishment, and grew. Water from a late fall rain fell into the crack, a norther froze it, and the expanding ice split the crack still wider. The growing juniper, over the many years, thickened its roots, pushing hard against the rock until it split, and the slab on the downhill side fell, turned over, and lay still.

The inner side of the slab was pressed tightly to the face of the slope. The exposed side, partly covered by the juniper roots, was seamed with bright streaks that ran like jagged lightning through the crumbling quartz.

A hundred years later, another coyote paused in the shade of the juniper, whose boughs now overhung the rock. He nibbled at some of the dry, hard-seeded fruits of the juniper, and rested for a while on the mat of leaves, berries, and shredded bark that had fallen from the tree.

It was in the fall of 1824 that a trapper crossing the arid slope toward the tree-clad mountains beyond the next valley, made a brief pause in the juniper shade. The dribble of water from the rock had widened the coyote-dug hole into a gully that at the top was several feet deep, and deepened steadily as it cut into the slope. This cut offered a shield for the fire he built to make coffee.

Seated over the dying coals, nursing his cup of coffee,

he idly sifted some rocks through his fingers. One fragment threw a tiny gleam into his eyes. Turning it in his fingers, he found the small rock was laced with a golden material.

The trapper had never seen gold except in the wedding ring of his mother, but he pocketed the nugget and forgot it when he moved off next morning.

For nineteen years he carried it for a pocket piece, believing it brought him luck. In 1843 he tossed the nugget into a trunk and settled down to running a tavern in a small Missouri town. He married, built a livery stable at the tavern, and forgot the nugget in the trunk. But within its tiny golden heart lay something explosive and violent, something that lay dormant now, but would one day shatter the Nevada-Utah nights with gunfire.

The trapper's tavern and livery stable brought him affluence, his wife brought him a son. In 1849 he supplied gold-seekers bound for California, but cholera swept the plains and he lost his wife and son.

Through all the years of success and sadness he remembered the land he had seen years before. It lived in his mind, and often with eyes closed he felt again the movement of a good horse, the sound of the wind in the grass or the cedars, the running water, the smell of dust and pines and gunpowder.

He remembered a land unpeopled and still, flecked with cloud shadow. He recalled the great red-walled canyons dotted with the deep green of cedar, or the high ridges golden with autumn's gift to the aspen. The towering, snowclad hills, the dancing mirage of the desert, the look of a Blackfoot's chest in the sights of a long Kentucky rifle, these he could not forget.

Finally he sold the tavern and the stable. He was a man growing old, but a man still strong, and a man who knew where his heart was. "You'll die out there, Jim," they warned him, and he smiled.

Of course ... on some dusty slope under the horns of a wounded buffalo or the claws of a grizzly on a mountain trail, or with an arrow in his guts. He might make his final stand on some lonely hill like an old bull, harried by wolves.

"Before I die, boys, I'll hear the wild geese call beyond the Green. I'll follow the tracks of elk and bear once more, smell the crushed cedar, and the hay of the wild meadows."

He emptied his glass and filled it again. "I like it here, but you've never seen the sun set over the Teton peaks, or looked across the vast beauty of House Rock Valley from the ridge. I'm sorry to leave you, boys, but I'm a-going back."

The trapper was camped on the Sweetwater before he mentioned the nugget to anyone. With him were four good men who had come together in the way such men will who have a common purpose, and a common feeling for the same things. They were all together that night, but the one he talked to was young Dick Felton.

Felton was the kind of young man he would have wished his son to be, a strong, fine man of courage and principle, who always did his share of what was to be done, and did not wait to be asked. It was Felton to whom he showed the nugget now.

"No question about it." Felton was positive, and he knew about such things. "That's gold. You locate that claim and you will have nothing to worry about."

The trapper tossed the nugget in his palm. "I will tell you boys where it is, and you can share and share alike. All I want from this country is what it is giving me now."

"It has been many years," said Felton. "Are you sure you can remember?"

"For a mountain man it is like walking to the corner store. Once you have been there, you can go back."

But the trapper did not live to see the place a second time. He was off on the flank of his party looking for game. He found an antelope, and the Utes found him. He got off one shot and went down fighting and calling them names in their own tongue. The warriors knew him, so they did not strip or mutilate the body.

Felton came upon the body when the grass was still fresh with morning, and they buried him on a sun-warmed southern slope with a cedar tree for a marker, and Felton led the way west.

A week later they lost Downey to another Ute raid, but Felton, Cohan, and Zeller went on their way to the trapper's mountain. They knew what to look for. From the spot where the trapper had picked up the nugget they would be able to look due west to the mountain peak with the glacier. It would be the tallest peak in sight.

Dan Cohan was a Dublin Irishman who had come west as Union Pacific track-layer, and had then become a teamster, and finally a miner. Zeller was a Dutchman, slow, powerful, stampeded by neither success nor failure. While one man of the three kept to high ground to look out for Indians, the others worked the dry washes for color.

Early in April Zeller took two pans from a bench on the inside bend of a wash, and both showed color. One fragment was rough, indicating it had come no great distance.

"I've got a feeling," Felton said that night in camp.

"Yah, idt looks goodt."

Cohan shrugged. "We've taken rough samples before."

It was noon when they found the place under a blue sky dotted with puffballs of cumulus that left small shadows on the hills. A ragged gully dropped half a mile down a slope into a wash, and Zeller showed them the pan. In the bottom were a dozen fragments, some of fair size, and all showing color. A second pan was even better.

Without comment, Zeller walked past the mouth of the gully and took a sample from the hollow under a rock. Gold, but very little ... two more pans further up tested nothing at all.

They were cautious men who had learned the hard

way. At daybreak the next day they worked up the gully, every pan showing good color. Shortly before noon Felton suggested a break, and he seated himself on a slab of rock in the shade of a gnarled and ancient cedar. He propped his feet against a rock and lit his pipe.

He smoked the pipe through, scanning the hills for signs of movement. Turning his head, he could look due west to the peak with the glacier. And then he leaned over to knock out his pipe, and there it was. A chunk of rock literally seamed with gold.

CHAPTER 2

Felton handed the quartz to Zeller while Cohan looked on. This was it, and they all knew it. While Zeller examined the rock, Felton began uncovering the broken slab. The quartz sparkled and shone.

"Jewelry rock," Cohan said, reverently.

Their hearts pounding, their mouths dry, they checked it out. Zeller took samples along the outcropping while Cohan paced it off. The title ledge was exposed almost to the crest, then reappeared on the other side.

Felton filled his pipe and kept his composure in spite of his excitement. "I'd better go to Carson. We will want a legal filing, and we will need supplies."

"I shall locadte the claims," Zeller said. "Dan is a bedter shot dan me. He vil standt guard."

Cohan walked back and, hands on hips, explained the nature of the outcropping and its extent. "Nothing to show until you break down inside, and then it is rich, just like here."

"All claims as equal partners. Right?" Felton said.

"Have you seen what happens?" Cohan asked. "They'll come a-runnin', the good and the bad."

"We will have a town," Felton agreed. "We must think

8

of that. We should choose a site, lay out some lots and a street."

Cohan indicated a bench two hundred yards down the slope. "There . . . how about that?"

Felton nodded. "I'll saddle up," he said. "It is a long ride to Carson."

It was a lonely, sun-blasted land. The mountains where their claims lay were cut by a myriad of canyons and arroyos, without pattern or system. Streams had formed them long ago, earthquakes had altered them, and then other streams had made their own changes.

Alone, Zeller and Cohan studied the land, kept watch for Utes, developed their claims, suffered the heat, and longed for the coolness of the distant mountain.

Three weeks to the day after his leave-taking, Felton returned. He rode into camp, and on the trail behind him they could see two big wagons, loaded with goods. The rush had begun.

The first wagon was in and half unloaded when Zeller pointed down the trail where a long cloud of dust hung in the still air. "Here dey coom. Now ve get idt."

"They'll come in handy if the Utes should come a-callin'," Cohan responded.

The first wagon was high-sided and covered with a tarp. The driver swung into the makeshift street, then he saw the staked lots. "What's those?" he demanded.

"City lots." Cohan replied, "and cheap at two hundred dollars the lot."

The driver was a portly man with a black mustache. The three men knew who he was, and they were glad to have him come. "You fellers ain't missin' much, are you?" he said, and he pointed toward the rough hillside with his whipstock. "I don't see any stakes there."

"Help yourself, Buckwalter," Felton said.

The man swung his team expertly into position, backed up and got down. The wagon canted at an angle, but he lowered the tail-gate, and with surprising ease swung one of the barrels into position. He hung a tin cup on the spigot.

"Two-bits a throw," he suggested.

Dan Cohan started to get up, but Buckwalter lifted a hand. "I want business, but not that bad. I just remembered. Big Thompson is in that crowd. If you've got yourself a good claim you'd better stay sober."

"Who is Big Thompson?" Felton asked.

"He never files a claim," Cohan said. "He just jumps one that is already proved, but you'd best not say that unless you've got a gun in your hand and somebody to cover your back."

"Doesn't anybody make a fight?"

"A few have tried it. None of them lasted very long."

"Iss no vun so fast, den?"

"Matt Coburn is," Buckwalter replied, "and he's a good man. I'd feel better if he was here. This is going to be his kind of town."

"This is our town," Felton said stiffly. "We will have no gunfighters here."

"You're dreamin'." Cohan spoke roughly. "I know this kind of crowd. So does Buckwalter. There will be some good minin' men, and there will be a lot of honest amateurs, but they'll be outnumbered by the rowdies, the gamblers, the killers, the sneak thieves, short-card artists, and cutthroats. There will be women in the crowd who have made every boom camp in the West, some of them tough enough to whip any two men in camp, and ready to do it."

"He's right," Buckwalter agreed. "I like your sentiments, son, but you can't pick an' choose.'

"We want a church and a school," Felton insisted. "We want a city council, and we want law and order."

Buckwalter glanced at Cohan. "Where's this boy been? He isn't dry behind the ears yet."

"He's a good man, Buck, and he will stand for what he believes."

"Then he'd better be good with a gun, too. Or else he'd better send for Coburn."

After a few minutes of silence, Buckwalter went on, "You will have one friend in the crowd who will stand hitched, Felton. Sturdevant Fife is coming up the trail with his printing press. He's a law-and-order man, and he runs his newspaper with a sawed-off shotgun on his desk."

Hundreds of belted men were coming up the trail, men booted, unshaved, and wild, coming up the highroad to hell. If they did not find their ticket in this town they would in the next.

Dusty and rough, they came in off the trail, riding horseback, driving wagons ... arriving by every kind of moving rig.

Within the hour Buckwalter had emptied his first barrel and sold it for thirty dollars to a gambler with a three-card monte game. Another man bought a lot, set up a tent, hung out his sign, and began selling miner's supplies.

"That's Jim Gage," Cohan said. "He never misses a boom town, he does a land-office business, then moves on. He's a good judge of booms, and when he sells out you know you're through. He will be a law-and-order man, too."

"How duss he know?" Zeller asked.

"Instinct, I guess. Anyway, when the roof falls in, he's always gone."

By nightfall three hundred men were camping or building along the slope. Of the twenty lots Zeller had staked out, twelve had been sold and two of them resold for bigger money.

It was just short of dark when four horsemen turned into the street and rode up to where Zeller and Felton sat. The man riding the lead horse was a huge bearded, burly man with small hard eyes.

Cohan stepped out, his Winchester in his hand, the muzzle holding on the big man's belt buckle. "You lookin' for somebody, Thompson?"

The big man stared hard, but the Irishman's eyes were steady. Thompson shifted his attention to Felton, who was also holding a rifle. Zeller, a little to one side, had removed a blanket from his shotgun.

"Just a place to camp." Thompson smiled affably. "I figured this was away from the noise and bustle."

"It's staked and filed land, Thompson."

"All we want is a place to camp."

"There was a Swede in Placerville who let you camp on his claim, an' when morning came he was gone. You said he'd sold you the claim and pulled out. I was there, Thompson. I helped dig up the body."

"Tell that story, and I'll kill you."

"I've told it. Now you start ridin'—right *now!*"

He eared back the hammer and Thompson stared at him, then spat. He turned slowly, taking his time, and went away down the slope, followed by the three other riders.

"He vill kill you if he can," Zeller said.

"We must have a town marshal," Felton said. "We can't have that sort of thing."

"You'll get no marshal. Not when they hear that Big Thompson and Peggoty Gorman are in town. They eat marshals for breakfast," Cohan said.

"They should be ordered out of town."

"Don't try it, Dick. I know you're game, but you're not that good and you're not that fast."

"And Coburn is?"

"If any man is."

"He'd be another Thompson, then."

"Not Matt Coburn," Buckwalter said. "I'd stake my life on him. In fact," he said wryly, "I already have. Several times."

Dick Felton watched the slope spring into life as lamps and lanterns were lighted, with here and there a campfire. One huge tent had just gone up, one of the tents such as housed the gambling hells that were to be found at the end of track when the Union Pacific was building. Men were still driving stakes, and already there was the sound of a music box from the tent, and the clink of glasses.

"Well," Cohan said, "you've got your town."

"We'll need a council. What do you say to Buckwalter?"

"All right. And Gage, if he will come in."

"I want you too, Dan."

"Take Zeller. He's a more cautious man."

"No." Zeller's refusal was definite. "I know not dees mans. Undt I must vork."

"Who else?"

"Fife, if you can get him. He may prefer to stay out, but even if he does you may get a name or two from him."

"The town should have a name."

Cohan chuckled. "By the look of it now, I can think of only one name—Confusion. Anyway, that's what they call these mountains."

"Confusion it is. But you'll see. It will be a different town in a few days."

Cohan glanced at Felton, but said nothing. There was no use trying to explain to a man from the East, even one as knowing and generally capable as Dick Felton. Even after you had seen a boom town you could not believe it. You had to live through a few of them, as he had.

Dawn broke to the sound of picks on the slope, and of hammers and saws in the town. Several wagons had brought dismantled buildings, which were now being raised into position, nailed together, and opened for business. The saloons, gambling houses, supply stores, and assayers were among the first.

With the money from the sale of lots, Felton hired three men to work with Zeller on their claims. Cohan and Felton took turns standing guard.

When Felton finished his shift as guard he went down the slope to talk to Sturdevant Fife. Pausing in the doorway to watch the street, he heard a sudden burst of gunfire.

A man, reeling and bloody, fell backwards from the door of the big gambling tent. He toppled into the dust, gun in hand, and struggled to rise. From the tent stepped a man in his shirt sleeves, a slender, handsome man with a cold, cruel face. Before the wounded man could rise, the gambler took careful aim and shot him through the head.

Felton started forward, but a hand from the tent caught his arm. It was Fife. "I know what you're thinkin', boy, but don't say it. He'll kill you."

"That was murder!"

"Keep your voice down, son. The dead man was armed, so they would never call it murder. You've got to remember when you pack a gun, you're fair game. That's Nathan Bly."

"Nathan Bly? *Here?*"

"Why not? He smells gold, boy. He's a gambler, and a good one. That dead feller probably thought he caught him cheatin'. Well, he never caught him. I ain't sayin' Bly wouldn't deal a few off the bottom if it suited him, but he's too good to get caught at it."

Felton followed Fife into the tent. He glanced at the type set up on the table:

... MEN KILLED ON THE FIRST DAY

"I'm leavin' the number open. The day ain't over yet."

"Fife, I want a city council of responsible men," Felton said. "Will you join us?"

"It ain't fitten, son. I want to stand clear to call names and tell you when you're wrong. But if you're right, I will say that too."

He studied the type through his steel-rimmed glasses, then looked at Felton over them. "There's a mighty lot about grammar that I don't know, and a lot of book learnin' I'll never have, but I know what I figure to be honest, and I'll say it.

"I found this here press in a cabin with the owner dyin' of a gunshot. He give it to me for buryin' him decent, with the promise that I tell the truth, the whole truth, and nothin' but the truth. That's what I've done."

"I like that," Felton replied. "And any time you think I am wrong, you say it."

For a few mintues there was silence. Somebody in the street was dragging the body of the dead man out of the way.

"We must have law here," Felton said. "Can you recommend anybody?"

"Can't help you, boy. I might want to call him names, or tell him he's done a wrong thing."

"I've heard about a man named Coburn."

"No."

Felton was surprised. "No?"

"Matt Coburn is a fine man, and maybe the best hand with a gun I ever did see, and I've seen a-plenty. He has nerve, but most of all he has judgment."

"Why not, then?"

"Matt's been like a son to me, and I don't like what this can do to him. You can't run a town like this without killin', an' I don't wish for Matt Coburn to kill anybody else."

On the fourth day Felton took a team and a borrowed plow and ripped up the street. Then with a drag borrowed from the same source, he graded the street as best he could, considering the rocks and the steepness of the hill.

"You'll get no thanks for that," Cohan said to him. "All they want is to get rich and get out."

Sturdevant Fife wrote an editorial about the grading, and demanded that all citizens try to keep the street free of bottles.

By the night of the fifth day there had been seven shootings, two of them fatal, and one man killed by a knife. Wilson, who had sold half of his claim to Big Thompson, disappeared.

"Got tired of it," Thompson said solemnly. "He's gone back to Washoe."

Every night there were fist fights, and shooting at all hours, and one tent set afire by a poor loser in a poker game.

Outside of town there was a hold up, and the stage—the first one that came into Confusion—was also held up and robbed.

And then Matt Coburn rode into town.

CHAPTER 3

He rode up the street in the freshness of morning before the sun was up, and he did not stop in the lower street, but rode on to the crest of the ridge, where he turned in his saddle to study the layout of the town and the country around.

Dick Felton was taking samples from that part of the Discovery claim that lay beyond the ridge, which was actually a second claim, known as Discovery II. He heard the horse, and looked around to see the rider outlined against the morning sky.

He was a tall young man, as tall as Felton himself, but heavier in the chest and shoulders. He wore a battered black hat, and a black coat over a faded red shirt. Felton could see the holster on his hip and what looked like the bulk of another six-shooter tucked behind his waistband.

"Any luck?" the rider asked.

"This is the Discovery claim, or part of it," Felton replied shortly. "It's a good one."

"You're Felton, then?"

"Yes." For some reason Felton was irritated. "What can I do for you?"

"I'm just passing by." He indicated the town. "I like to look at new towns, to wonder how long they will last."

17

"This one will."

"Maybe. Silver and gold are unreliable—they come and they go. It takes more than a mine to make a town."

"What it takes," Felton replied, "we've got."

The stranger laughed, and Felton started to speak angrily, then swallowed his irritation and picked up his samples and pick.

The rider had started to move off, but he drew up and indicated the mountain with the glacier. "I like that. I think that's where I'll go."

Felton looked toward the mountain. He had often looked upon it during the past few days. "That's where the trapper was going who first found gold here," he commented. "He wasn't even sure it was gold."

"What he found over there would be better. Is there anyone there?"

"I doubt it. I heard there was some woman had a cattle outfit at the foot of the hills, but that's unlikely. This is Ute country.'

"You never can tell about a woman. Some of them have more built-in nerve than a body would expect."

Without a backward glance, he rode away, and Felton went back to camp. Cohan was frying meat. He indicated the rider with a bob of his head. "What did he have to say?"

"He's riding on."

"Well, you met him, anyway."

"Met who? He didn't offer his name."

"That was Matt Coburn."

Felton sat down abruptly. *Matt Coburn!*

"I'm sorry to see him go," Cohan said. "He's a good man, and before this is over we'll need him the worst way."

"We don't want him. Not his kind.'

Cohan merely shrugged and went to the pot for coffee. Felton still felt irritated. Suppose this was his first boom town? There was violence, but he had expected that. He had worked in timber-cutting crews as a boy, and he knew about a rough crowd. He said as much.

"The trouble is," Cohan replied, "those boys you knew didn't pack six-shooters. You'll find some of that lot here too, but they're pretty small potatoes."

Matt Coburn held to no trail, preferring to make his own way into the Snake Valley. He was not in any hurry, and he had no destination, which was just the trouble. There never had been a destination, and a man just had to be heading for something, somewhere, if he figured to amount to anything.

Yet it was not strictly true. Back there before the war, when he was a youngster he had dreams of becoming a lawyer. He had saved his money and bought a copy of Blackstone . . . what ever became of it, anyway?

When the war was over he had to make a living. He worked for a freight outfit on the Santa Fe Trail, then as a shotgun messenger for Wells Fargo.

For five months he had no trouble, while others were robbed, or robberies were attempted. Then one night, not far from Sand Mountain, they surprised him.

He dropped to the ground and opened fire, and when the fireworks were over he was packing two slugs, but one bandit was dead, another seriously wounded, and the third he tracked down and brought in on the very stage he had tried to hold up.

One week later he had walked out on the street for the first time and three of the outlaws' friends were waiting for him. They had him boxed, and expected him to drop his gunbelt on command. Instead, he drew. It caught them flatfooted, and in a matter of seconds he had chalked up his second and third killings. The third man escaped, carrying a bullet as a memento of the occasion.

Coburn drew his time and drifted to Colorado, where he hired out as a cowhand. Four months later he went to Texas to drive a herd to Dodge. After one scramble with rustlers and two Kiowas, he brought the cattle in, and went after a second herd, which he bought with his own money. The Kiowas were waiting for him and he lost his head and his shirt.

For four months he was a deputy marshal in a cow town and never drew a gun on a man. He had a reputation for being fair and the trail hands knew he'd come up from Texas himself, so when he talked, they listened. But he was restless, and he moved on.

He was still moving on, partly because he liked the look of the mountains ahead of him and partly because he knew what was happening in the town behind him. He knew every move that had been made, and those that would be made. Even some of the names were the same.

He saw the rider before she saw him. She was a quarter of a mile down the slope, and a hundred yards ahead of him. She was riding a blazed-face sorrel, and she carried a rifle as if she intended to use it.

Coburn, from higher up, could see the two men she was following. One was Kid Curtis, a small-time gunman and cow thief; the older man was Skin Weber. He had been around Pioche, Virginia City, and Eureka, always running with the rough bunch. Neither man had ever raised a cow in his life.

Replacing his field glasses in his saddlebag. Coburn angled across the slope, keeping to the cover of the scattered juniper when possible. He had a notion that girl would need help when she caught up with her cattle.

His approach brought him to the cut through the hills before the cattle could make it. He wasted no time examining his motives. The necessity for action was here and he accepted the responsibility. Had the pursuer been a man he would have left him to his own devices, but no woman was fitted to cope with Weber and Curtis.

The cattle were a good-looking lot, longhorns crossed with some other breed that gave them more beef. The two riders hazed them into the cut. "Somebody comin'," Weber said.

Matt knew it was his own horse that Weber's horse had sensed, but neither man suspected Matt's presence.

Skin walked back to the opening and looked down the trail. "You're right—somebody comin'. Looks like that Shannon girl."

"You can't shoot a woman," Curtis replied.

"Kid, sometimes you're a damn fool. Who'd shoot a good-lookin' woman at a time like this?"

Curtis glanced at him uneasily. "Skin ... you watch it. Nobody in his right mind fools around with a woman in this country."

Skin's reply was a dry chuckle. "She's a long way from home, and she's got no husband to worry over what becomes of her."

"She's got a couple of cowhands. They could become almighty curious. We left a trail a blind man could foller."

"Uh-huh, an' from here on we leave no trail a-tall."

A sudden silence cause Matt to peer around the slab of rock behind which he was hidden. The girl had ridden into the cut, and it was obvious she had not expected anyone to be waiting there. Her rifle started to lift, but she was already under their guns.

"I have been following my cattle," she said. She was very cool. "They seem to have drifted off my range."

Skin was amused. "Ma'am, they didn't drift. We pushed 'em. The boys up yonder at the mines need beef."

Kid Curtis was worried. Matt could see it in the way he kept licking his lips and looking from the girl to Weber.

"They are my cattle, gentlemen, and I shall drive them back to my ranch." She was not only cool, she was hard. She did not seem the least bit frightened. But Matt was alert to her danger.

"Well, if you ain't a gonna be reasonable—" Skin put his rifle down. "Kid, if she makes one wrong move, you shoot her, d'you hear? Don't mess her up, just shoot her

in the shoulder or the knee like. We kind of want her
the way she is."

Matt Coburn stepped from behind the rock. His rifle
was in the saddle scabbard, and he had not drawn a
pistol. But he had to stop it before the girl tried to shoot,
which he knew she would do.

Skin started toward her, and at that instant she saw
Matt Coburn. Her sudden start of surprise made Curtis
turn his head. "Skin," he warned, "we got trouble."

"Aw, most of em fight a little bit until they find out
who's boss. I'll just—"

"Skin!" The sharpness of Curtis' tone stopped Weber.
"We got compn'y."

Skin Weber did not like interruptions. He had his own
plans, and he was angry. Then his eyes followed the
Kid's.

He looked at Matt Coburn and did not like what he
saw. "Where'd you come from?"

"Skin . . . be careful."

The warning in Curtis' tone was obvious, and it rang
an alarm in Weber's brain that burned through his anger. "Whoever you are, get out! Get out whilst you're
able."

Matt Coburn let a slow moment go by. "I was going
to make you that offer, Skin, but after your attitude
toward the young lady here, I don't much care whether
you go or stay. The buzzards will have you boys sooner
or later, and it might as well be here."

Skin Weber was suddenly cautious. This man was cool
and confident; he was unworried. In the world in which
Skin Weber moved, that meant the stranger had an
edge. Skin's eyes swept the rocks. Were other men hidden here?

His eyes went back to Coburn. This man could have
drawn his gun before he stepped into sight, but he had
not. That meant he believed he could get into action fast
enough, and that might mean that he was somebody.
But Skin Weber himself was a handy man with a gun
and he did not like backing down.

"We're just havin' a little fun. You beat it."

Coburn's attitude did not change. "Skin, you've got the lady's cattle. You stole them from her ranch."

"You callin' me a cow thief?" Skin's tone held a threat.

"Sure I am, Skin. You've been called one before. You've also been called a horse thief, a dry-gulching murderer, and a robber of drunks and old ladies."

Skin was appalled. The man was deliberately goading him into making a fight of it. And the more eager the man was for a fight, the less eager Skin became.

"Skin"—Kid Curtis spoke only loud enough for his ears—"that's Matt Coburn."

Laurie Shannon was looking at Skin Weber when the Kid spoke, and she saw the face of a man who had looked upon death. Slowly and carefully, Weber eased his hand away from his gun.

It was Curtis who spoke. "Mister, if it's all the same to you, we'd like to ride out of here."

"All right, boys, if you want to ride . . . ride."

Kid Curtis walked stiff-legged to his hose. He did not look to see if Weber followed. Only when he was in the saddle did he look back. Skin had not stirred, and the paleness of his face had given way to the red of anger.

"Skin," Curtis said, "don't try it."

A moment more Weber hesitated, then slowly he turned away. Curtis watched warily, his own hands clasped very plainly on the pommel.

Skin mounted and the two gunmen rode out of the cut, with Matt Coburn following to see that they continued to travel.

"Mr. Coburn, I would like to thank you."

When the girl spoke, he turned and looked squarely at her for the first time, and he thought that she was beautiful. She had auburn hair and hazel eyes, and she was taller than most women.

"You will need help to drive the cattle back," he said. "May I lend a hand?"

They had started the cattle when two riders appeared, charging up in a cloud of dust from pounding hoofs. One was young, aggressive, and somewhat arrogant. The second man was nearing fifty, with careful blue eyes that missed nothing. He had a look of seasoned toughness about him.

"You all right?" he asked the girl.

"Mr. Coburn helped me. I'm afraid I rode into trouble, Joss."

"Coburn?" The young one turned sharply for a better look. "*Matt* Coburn?"

"That's the name," Matt replied, then ignored him. He knew the type. A tied-down gun and some swagger about him. A fresh one who had yet to learn that it needs more than a gun to make a gunfighter.

"It's all right," Coburn told the older man. "No trouble."

"Where are they? Did you shoot 'em?" That was the younger one again, asking questions instead of listening and learning.

"Why shoot them?"

"You mean they just *gave* you the cattle? That was Kid Curtis and Skin Weber. I got close enough to spot 'em."

"They misread the brands," Coburn replied solemnly. "They said they were sorry."

"*Sorry?* An' you let 'em get away? Why, I'd have—"

"Got yourself shot more'n likely." The older man was patient. "Thank you, Coburn. You saved us some grief."

"*Por nada*," Coburn said, smiling. "I'll be riding on."

"Wait," the girl said quickly. "I'm Laurie Shannon, and I own the Rafter LS. We don't have much of an outfit yet, but we set a good table. Will you come along and take potluck with us?"

She indicated the older man. "This is Joss Ringgold, and ... Freeman Dorset."

"Howdy."

Ringgold ... he knew the name. A salty old-timer who would stand hitched, but there was trouble in the young one. If he could keep that gun in his holster until he was old enough to know when to use it, he might live as long as Ringgold, but Coburn would have taken no bets on it.

"There's no place to eat within twenty miles," Joss suggested, "unless you go back to Confusion."

Coburn hesitated, for he had learned to be wary of human relationships. He had learned the hard way that men could not be trusted too much. All men—and women—were sadly, weakly human. They were inclined to expect more than they were likely to get, and to expect it to come easier.

"All right," he said, and immediately regretted it. He had often made a lonely camp, and had not minded it too much. He could have done so again.

There was trouble in the quiet, strong young beauty of Laurie Shannon, and there was trouble in Dorset. About Joss Ringgold he had no worries. He and Ringgold spoke the same language, they had eaten the dust, felt the rain, branded calves on the open grass, and they had bitten on the bullet.

Meanwhile, back in Confusion, circumstances were moving men on the chessboard to involve Matt Coburn.

For there are, in the affairs of men and nations, inexorable tides from which they cannot remain aloof. If they do not enter upon them prepared, they will be caught unprepared, and at the wrong time.

All Matt Coburn wanted just now was a good meal, and by such small motives are the lives of men altered.

CHAPTER 4

By evening of the seventh day there were five tent saloons in Confusion, and two frame buildings were under construction. There were three stores, a blacksmith shop, a tent theatre, two tent hotels, and about three dozen dugouts, shacks, and tents for private residences. At least a hundred men were camping without shelter.

After a meeting at Gage's place the council had chosen a marshal, a respected, well-liked ex-soldier named McGuinness.

Outside on the street, Felton said, "Well, Dan, I feel better now. We'll have some law. McGuinness is a good man."

Dan Cohan offered no comment, and Zeller and Buckwalter were lighting their cigars. Finally Cohan did speak. "He'll be lucky," he said, "if he lasts out the week."

Dick Felton stared at him. "That's one hell of a thing to say!"

"Dan's right," Buckwalter said. "You don't know what's coming. McGuinness is too good a man to have this happen to him."

"To have what happen? What are you talking about?"

"He isn't tough enough, Dick. McGuinness is a brave

26

man, but bravery isn't enough. Gun skill isn't enough. For this lot you have to be *tough*."

"They've busted marshals in twenty towns," Buckwalter said.

Felton stifled his annoyance. McGuinness was tough.

They would see soon enough.

He walked up the hill to their claim with Zeller and Cohan. They had been sleeping in the open under the stars, but today they had begun to dig into the side of the ridge. It was only a beginning, but they would dig out a room, and then use rocks from the claim to build another room in front.

From up here the lights of the town were clear and bright. He could hear the sounds of a piano and of a music box, and occasionally a raucous yell sounded, or the shrill laughter of a girl.

McGuinness would handle it, all right. He was a good man. He had been a sergeant during the War Between the States, he was used to rough men, and was a good shot.

Suddenly a door slammed, and the night was split by a stab of flame and a shot, followed by a cannonade of several shots in rapid succession. Felton started toward the trail but Cohan caught his arm. "Don't go," he said.

"But that was no drunken miner!" Felton protested. "That was a gun battle. Maybe McGuinness is in trouble."

"Maybe he is," Cohan replied, "but you'd better not go down there unless you are armed and prepared to fight."

Felton hesitated, and Zeller added his comment. "Idt vill keep undtil morning, I t'ink."

There were no more shots. Somebody was talking loudly in the streets, and after a few minutes they heard footsteps on the trail. Cohan stepped back inside and picked up Zeller's shotgun and their rifles and passed them out.

They could see several men were coming. One of them, judging by size alone, must be Big Thompson.

"All right," Felton said, "just hold it right there."

"You ain't hospitable, Mr. Felton." Thompson's voice was teasing, and it angered Felton to think the man thought so little of him. "We come to make you an offer. My partners an' me, we figured you might sell us a workin' share in your claim."

"Don't be foolish," Felton replied brusquely.

"Figured you might," Thompson drawled, "as things are changin' around here. An' you needin' a sheriff, and all."

"We have a sheriff."

Thompson chuckled. "You had one. He made a mistake. He tried to draw agin me. That's almost as big a mistake as tryin' to fist-fight me."

"You've killed him?"

"Nothin' else we could do," Thompson said innocently. "He was interferin' with the free conduct of our pleasures, an' he went for his gun when pushed. . . . You think about it, gents. I'd give you a hundred dollars for a fourth share."

"You're crazy! This claim's worth a million."

"Maybe . . . maybe not. How much is it worth to a dead man?"

The sound of a cocking hammer was loud in the night. "All right, Thompson. You've made your point. Now get down the hill before we dig another grave alongside the sheriff's."

Thompson chuckled again, then turned slowly away, and with the others walking beside him, he went down the hill.

For several minutes after their departure nobody spoke, and then it was Zeller who said, "Ve haff godt to do somet'ings."

At daybreak Buckwalter, Gage, Wayne Simmons, and Newton Clyde had come up the hill to talk. Simmons operated a freighting and stage business; Newton Clyde was the Wells Fargo man.

"Get Coburn," Clyde said abruptly. "He knows this crowd and they know him."

"No," Felton said flatly. "I won't have him."

"How about it, Buckwalter? Who would you suggest?"

"Well, if Coburn is out, we might try Calvin Bell. I hear he's over to Durango. He ran a couple of Kansas trail towns."

A rider was coming up the trail. He was a stocky man, unshaven and dirty. With him were two others, both as thin as laths, sour, evil-looking men.

The stocky man drew up alongside the group where they sat on the dump outside the Discovery hole. "Hear you folks are needin' a marshal. Me an' my boys would take the job. We kin run your town. I'm Hick Sutton, an' these are my boys, Sam an' Joe."

"No," Felton said.

"Wait a minute, Dick." Cohan looked up at Sutton. "What makes you think you can run a tough town?"

"We run a few places in our time. I want two hundred a month. A hundred apiece for the boys here."

"That's pretty steep," Gage objected.

"You got trouble. We can handle it. How much is cheap?"

"Ever hear of Big Thompson?"

Sutton grinned. "He's a man, ain't he? I'll handle him."

"All right," Newton Clyde said. "You run Thompson and Peggoty Gorman out of town and you've got the job."

Sutton looked at the others. "You agree to that?"

Gage nodded, then Buckwalter. Reluctantly, Felton agreed.

Sutton wheeled his horse. "You want to gimme that badge? I'll need some authority."

Cohan handed him McGuinness' badge, which Gage had brought with him up the hill. The three rode off, laughing.

Felton, Cohan, and Zeller returned to work on the claim, and the others to their businesses. But each man listened, expecting the sound of gunfire.

"We're out of beef," Cohan commented. "One of us should ride out and shoot some meat."

"There's a ranch over west of here," Felton commented. "We might be able to buy a side of beef there."

Cohan grinned at Zeller. "See? He's heard the story, too."

Felton tried to look surprised. "What story?"

"About that pretty girl who's ramrodding that outfit. If you want to stay a bachelor, Dick, you'd better fight shy of girls. You're a moneyed man now."

Felton saddled up and rode off and the others settled down to work.

Below them the town slowly awakened. A stage filled with sleepy passengers rolled up to the stage station and several men and women got down stiffly, the men stamping their clothes into shape, the women fluffing, brushing, and straightening theirs.

The air was cool and fresh. Down the street in front of the Bon-Ton a man lay sprawled on the boardwalk. Another sat on a bench close by, fast asleep, his chin on his chest.

Wayne Simmons, a cigar in his teeth, watched the passengers get down. The driver stepped over to him and said in a low tone. "He was out there again today, keepin' out o' sight, but watchin' us. I figure he's waitin' for a gold shipment or somethin'."

"All right. I'll get a man to ride shotgun."

"Get a good one," the driver said. "I don't relish bein' shot at."

A man emerged from Buckwalter's National Saloon and began to sweep off the board porch. Beyond him a tall, slim man in a gray tailored suit appeared on the walk. He strolled up the street and stopped beside Simmons.

"Howdy, Nathan," Simmons said. "How're the cards treating you?"

"They always treat me well, Wayne. I'm a careful man. The cards respect that in a gambler."

The two men watched the passengers going into the

restaurant, and then Nathan Bly took out a cigar. "I received a notice a few minutes ago."

"A notice?"

"It was a notice from the marshal's office of a ten per cent charge on all gambling games, payable to the marshal or his deputies."

"This is the first I've heard of it."

"I had an idea that was the way it was. I'm glad to hear the town council had nothing to do with it. I don't mind paying something to build boardwalks, to keep the town clean, or to build a church or a schoolhouse, but I don't like a shakedown."

"I'll speak to that marshal. I'll speak to him right away."

Nathan Bly smiled slightly. "Do it before he tries to collect, will you? I don't like to get my floor messed up."

Bly turned and strolled away, slender, elegant, but no man to buy trouble with. Wayne Simmons turned toward the restaurant for his morning coffee when he saw Buckwalter coming. By the very look of him Simmons knew that Buckwalter had received the word, too.

They discussed it over breakfast. "Forget it," Buckwalter said after a bit. "If he can collect from Bly, he'll deserve it."

"I don't like it, Buck. I don't like it at all."

Dick Felton found the trail to the Rafter LS and rode up to the ranch shortly before noon. Tied to the hitch rail in front of the house there was a big appaloosa that looked familiar. Swinging down, he walked up to the door and rapped.

Laurie Shannon answered the door. "Oh . . . I'm Laurie Shannon. What can I do for you?"

Felton was embarrassed. "I'm from Confusion. I wanted to buy some beef."

She stepped back. "Come in. I'm just having some coffee with Mr. Coburn."

Felton stiffened slightly, and would have drawn back, but Laurie had walked on into the kitchen and picked up the coffeepot and a cup. As she filled the cup she turned, "Mr. Coburn . . . Mr.—"

"Felton, Dick Felton. I own the Discovery."

"We've met, I think," Matt said. He was relaxed and cool. Felton did not feel relaxed, and he was certainly not cool. He sat down abruptly.

"How are things in Confusion?" Coburn asked

"Fine . . . just fine. We hired a new marshal this morning, and two deputies. A man named Hick Sutton."

Coburn chuckled, but without humor. "You better enjoy him," he said. "He picked the wrong town and you won't have him long."

"Do you know him?"

"Sure. He's a thief and a high-binder. He takes the job as marshal and uses the badge for a right to shake down the gamblers. If he gets away with that, he moves on to legitimate businessmen. If anybody refuses, they have an accident . . . or they get shot . . . dry-gulched."

"I don't believe that."

There was silence in the room, and when Felton looked up, Coburn's eyes were on him. "You have lived long enough to know, Felton, that you've said the wrong thing."

Felton was about to explode into anger when he realized where he was, and what he had said.

"I did not mean it that way, Coburn," he said, "but don't get the idea that I am afraid of you."

"I don't think you are, and there's no reason why you should be." Matt Coburn got up. "Laurie, I'll go check out those steers on Wildcat."

At the door he paused. "Nice to have seen you again, Felton."

When the door closed, Dick Felton sipped his coffee to cover his irritation. He had made a fool of himself.

"Will you have some more coffee?" Laurie Shannon asked quietly.

Felton pushed his cup toward her and looked up. "I guess that sounded pretty bad."

"I've known men to get shot for less," Laurie said,

"and from all I've heard Matt Coburn isn't the man to take an insult."

"I didn't mean it that way," he said, "but he wants the job as marshal himself, so he'd naturally be ready to say something to prejudice me against Sutton."

"I don't believe so, Mr. Felton. And I happen to know that Matt Coburn does not want to be marshal of your town. He has no intention of going back there. At the moment he is planning to go to California, but I am trying to persuade him to start ranching here in the mountains."

"Ranching? *Him?*"

"Why not? He grew up on a cattle ranch, and has handled some big drives. He knows men, cattle, horses, and grazing conditions. In fact, he's taught me more in the past couple of days than I believed I could learn from anyone."

Felton still felt nettled. Why should Matt Coburn have stopped here, of all places? He directed the conversation back to beef cattle, then to Laurie Shannon herself, and discovered that she had been born in Ireland, but had grown up in Pennsylvania and Oregon.

He looked around him curiously. For such a time and place the house was large, and was comfortably built. There were four big rooms, and provision for two more to be added. Outside were a log barn and corrals, with a spring behind the house. A small stream flowed down from the glacier. The site had been carefully chosen, the building planned for beauty as well as efficiency.

The afternoon was drawing on. Reluctantly, he got up to leave.

"I'll send Free and Joss over with the cattle in the morning," Laurie said.

"Is Coburn working for you?" Felton asked.

"He doesn't work for anyone right now. He has been helping around since he's been here, but that's his own idea. He helped me out of a rather bad situation a few days ago, and I think he likes the food." She smiled as she added the last bit.

Matt Coburn rode into the yard as Felton was mounting. "I am sorry I spoke the way I did," Felton told ing. "We lost our marshal and Sutton replaced him."

"I heard about it. You know, Felton, these towns all follow a pattern. They are born in violence and struggle. Often they die the same way. Sometimes the towns last. Those that do are usually pacified by violence. When the rough element finds it can't win, it moves on. The stable ones stay and the town grows. Then it depends on whether the mines hold up, and whether other industries develop. But first you have to bring peace to the town, and the Suttons have never brought anything but robbery, murder, and terror.

"However," he added before Felton could speak, "I wouldn't worry too much about them. When they try to collect their shakedown money they'll run into trouble. They may know some western towns, but they don't know Nathan Bly, Buckwalter, or Newton Clyde."

"What do you mean by that?"

Coburn smiled. "You watch what happens. Those Sutton boys are mean, rotten clear through, and dangerous . . . just the kind that Nathan Bly eats for breakfast."

Dick Felton rode back to Confusion in the cool of an evening that soon changed to night, with the stars out. He did not ride up the main trail into the town, but chose a back trail that brought him over the crest onto his own claims. Dan Cohan challenged him as he came up the slope.

"It's me Dan. Everything all right?"

"There's been hell to pay down in town. The Suttons killed Lopez . . . you know, the one who started that saloon at the end of the street. Lopez came out into the street after Sutton, and the two boys were waiting with their rifles. He never had a chance."

"And then what?"

"They figured they had the town buffaloed. Joe and Sam Sutton went into Bly's place to collect. Bly laughed at them and they went for their guns. Both of them are dead."

"What about Hick Sutton?"

"Peggoty Gorman and Kid Curtis got the drop on him. They took his guns away and then Big Thompson gave him a beating. The worst thing I ever saw. Finally they pinned his star to the seat of his pants and ran him out of town, whipping him with their ropes and quirts."

Dick Felton sat down abruptly. He had been wrong, and the others had been right. He had been too stubborn to admit even to himself that things could go so badly. He had grown up in an ordered community where most of the citizens had respect for law and order. There were stories about the old days, of course, when things had been otherwise, but nothing like this. Here the forces of violence were completely in command.

He had thought of this as his town. He had led the others here, following the old trapper's story, and together they had discovered gold, but from that time on nothing had gone as it should. Moreover, their two victories would only give the outlaw elements greater confidence.

He was perfectly prepared to defend his claim, as were Zeller and Cohan. The three men working for them were armed and prepared to fight; but to defend the claim was one thing, to defend the town was another.

Newton Clyde came up the hill. Wells Fargo had as yet no office in the town, so he had nothing to defend. Buckwalter, Gage, and the others were afraid to leave their businesses for fear of what might happen. There was no unity—there were only scattered islands of defense.

"Coburn's our man," Clyde said positively. "I know of nobody else I'd trust. Gage and Buckwalter think the same."

"Why him? Why only Coburn?"

"Felton, with all due respect, you wouldn't last an hour down on that street. Neither would I. It takes a special kind of man to go down there, with a special kind of mind and a very special kind of conditioning. Above all, he's got to know what he's up against.

"These mining towns aren't like the Kansas cow towns. The men they are up against here aren't like the Texans, who in most cases want to meet you face to face. Some of these men are that way, but most of them are back-shooters, dry-gulchers, murderers. They're thoroughly vicious. They aren't just rough men driving cattle across the plains to sell; these men come here to kill, to murder.

"There's good men down in that town, and there are some of the best miners in the world. They are honest men, but each one of them is alone. Right now I'd guess there are two to three thousand men in this camp, and at least half of them are the worst lot in the world. I saw three down there who used to run with the Sydney Ducks on the Barbary Coast; they were convicts sent out to Australia who escaped and came to this country. There's two more who I know did time in Yuma prison, and there are Wanted posters out on a dozen more."

"Coburn is on his way to California," Felton said. "I don't think he'd take the job."

"You've talked to him?"

"Uh-huh—today over at Laurie Shannon's. I imagine he's still there."

"We'd better get him, then. There's nobody else who can handle that bunch. Look, staying up here on the hill you can only hear it. I live with it.

"There was a knifing last night, and later two men were cheated at cards, and when they complained they were ordered out—at gun point. A big winner at the Nugget was knocked on the head and robbed before he got to the end of the street. You'll hear about it before night; I heard it a few minutes ago.

"About twenty roughnecks raided the sluiceboxes at the Joy Boy. It's back up the wash about half a mile and they've got a good placer operation there. This bunch pushed in, held Peterson and his son under a gun, cleaned up the sluices, and took all they could find in the cabin, even his guns, ammunition, and food. They rode off whooping."

"I don't believe in running a town with a gun," Felton said, "There's got to be another way."

"You think of it, then," Clyde said, "but make out your last will and testament before you try it. Believe me, Thompson isn't the worst of them down there. There's a dozen that are as bad, and half a dozen that are worse."

"How about this Calvin Bell I've heard of?"

"He's good with a gun—maybe as good as Matt, although I have my doubts. But he's cruel, dangerous. His gun is for hire, and he'd work for a bad outfit as quick as for a good one. Matt wouldn't."

"Would Bell sell out?"

"No. He's not that kind. Once he's sold, he stays sold."

"Well, how about him?"

"It would take him a week to get here. Another thing— he hates Matt Coburn. And anyway, you don't want that kind of man."

"In a week that outfit could destroy all we've built," Cohan said. "Listen to them."

Shouts and yells came from down the street, punctuated by occasional gunshots. It was odd, Felton thought, how after a while you could distinguish between the shots fired by some casual drunk celebrating and the shots that meant business.

The mind had a peculiar way of discriminating between sounds. He had watched the old trapper when the wind was in the trees making all manner of rustling— the squeaking of branches, the stirring among the leaves; and then the old man would pick out of it all the sound of a deer moving, or a man or a bear or whatever. Felton's own mind had developed some of this instinct by the time he had arrived here.

"It's Coburn then," he said. "Get him if you can—I've no objections."

After some talk it was decided that Felton would go after him, accompanied by Newton Clyde.

"It won't be easy," Felton said. "He sounded positive—and he may already have gone on west."

Did he really believe that? Or was the wish father to the thought?

CHAPTER 5

The town of Confusion basked in the warm sun. There were the unceasing sounds of hammer and saw. Confusion was building. A placer miner down the wash reported values of thirty to thirty-five cents to the pan. Two experienced miners from Virginia City reported a showing of silver on the crest of a ridge a quarter of a mile back up the canyon.

In the saloons there was talk of ore, of great discoveries. Every prospector is by nature an optimist, any hole in the ground is a potential bonanza. Over at Hamilton a man had taken $3,000,000 from a hole seventy feet wide and at no point more than twenty-eight feet deep. Two men had thrown up a rock house for shelter from the cold winds and found its walls contained $75,000 worth of ore. Out in California a report told of a nugget of solid gold weighing over one hundred pounds. Nothing was impossible nor even improbable.

Every stage that came into Confusion brought prospectors, some to search the hills for gold or silver, some to mine it from the pockets of the miners. They came with picks and shovels, or they came with marked cards or guns.

Every few steps there was a saloon, and in every saloon there was a wheel or card tables, or both. There were men who had made every boom camp from Virginia City, Nevada, to Virginia City, Montana. They had worked over the green felt tables from the Mother Lode country of California to Cherry Creek in Colorado. They knew the names of all the town "chiefs," those gunmen who ruled the towns for a while and then went down before faster guns, or luckier ones. "Farmer" Peel, John Bull, Eldorado Johnny, Sam Brown, Tom Lahey, Blue Dick, and Morgan Courtney—the names were different from those known to the Kansas trail towns, but the endings of the men were the same.

By the fifteenth day in the life of Confusion, there had been seven killings, nine robberies, and two stage holdups. Nobody bothered to count the number of drunks rolled, or the minor fights with fists, knives, or guns that did not end in death.

The Discovery claim was proving rich. They had found gold, and they were also finding silver, as had happened on the Comstock and in the San Juan country.

"I'll ship your gold," Newton Clyde told them, "if Matt Coburn rides shotgun."

But nobody had ridden over to the Rafter LS to see if Matt was still in the country. Neither Felton nor his partners dared leave the claim, with so much gold on hand. One of them sat over it every minute, shotgun in hand, with another loaded rifle nearby. It was commonly talked around that in the short time the claim had been worked it had produced thirty thousand in gold. If that was truth or only rumor nobody would say.

Down below them in the town, along the street of saloons, gambling tents mingled with a scattering of stores, a blacksmith shop, a gunsmith, and two wide-open dance halls, as well as businesses and dwellings of all sorts.

Wagons and riders still streamed into the town. Holdups and murders along the road into town were frequent—or so it was reported. Nobody even rode out to verify most of the stories.

Matt Coburn was scouting the eastern slopes of the Fortification Range. For days he had done little but prowl through the canyons of the Snake, Fortification, and Wilson Creek ranges. They were rugged mountains, pine-clad and beautiful. Two nights he camped out in the lonely cabins, keeping a wary eye for Utes. Finally, he turned his horse back toward the Rafter LS.

Laurie Shannon was watering flowers when he rode into the yard. She straightened, shading her eyes against the sun.

"Well! I was wondering what had happened to you."

"Scouting," he said. "I like the country."

"Come inside. There's coffee on, and we've some fresh doughnuts.'

He seated himself at the kitchen table with its red-and-white checked cloth and watched her as she poured coffee and set out a plate of doughnuts. He crossed his legs and hung his hat over his knee, his eyes taking in the china and the polished copper. It was a warm, pleasant room.

"I've known cowhands to ride sixty or seventy miles because they heard somebody was making doughnuts," he said. "We used to call them bear-sign."

They talked aimlessly of grass, cattle, and the mountains, while the shadows crept down the mountainside and filled the hollow. Laurie got up to light the coal-oil lamp. "I've got to clean the chimney," she commented, "and trim that wick."

When she sat down again she said, "They're having trouble in Confusion. It's a rough, tough crowd."

"Pioche was the worst. They buried seventy-five men before there was one that died of natural causes. All these boom towns go through a period of violence, but when the bad element is moved out they settle down. Only some of them never survive the change."

"It's a pity."

"I know that crowd," Coburn mused, "or their type. That's part of the business of running such towns—to know those who are really bad from the ones who are merely blowing off steam, or the kids itching for a reputation but who right down at the bottom don't want to take a chance on getting killed to earn it." He was silent for a few minutes. "I want no more of that. I want to go to ranching."

"You mean all my arguments haven't been wasted?"

He smiled. "What else could a drifter think of? Some drifters do it just for the drifting, others just wander around looking for a place to light. I guess that fits me."

"And you've chosen this place?"

He looked at her. "You chose it for me."

There was a little color in her face. "I'd like to have you close by. I worry, sometimes, about Indians."

"I was meaning to mention that. You shouldn't keep so much food in sight. Do you have a cellar?"

"No."

"Get somebody busy. It might be good for Dorset," he suggested, "if he'll stand for it. Anyway, dig a cellar and store your food in it. Indians will eat all there is in sight—they'll stuff themselves. It doesn't do any harm to feed them, but it's best to have only a little food out in sight, and make them think that's all you have."

They heard the riders coming, and Matt Coburn hitched his chair back into deeper shadow. A moment later there was a tap at the door and Joss Ringgold spoke. "Ma'am? It's some folks from Confusion. They're huntin' Coburn . . . an' they're friendly."

Another voice said, "It's Dick Felton, Miss Shannon. And Newton Clyde, of Wells Fargo."

She opened the door. "Come in, gentlemen. You know Matt Coburn, I think."

Felton nodded, and Clyde stepped forward, holding out his hand. "How are you, Matt? It's been a long time."

When they were seated, Matt looked across the table at Clyde. "What is it, Newt? I know you didn't ride all this way just for fun."

"We've got a shipment . . . a big one. Most of it is from Mr. Felton's Discovery. I want you to ride shotgun."

"Who's driving?"

"Dandy Burke . . . need I say more?"

"He's a good man. How far do you want me to ride?"

"All the way. To Carson City. There's fifty dollars in it, Matt."

"No."

Newton Clyde was surprised. "Matt, fifty dollars isn't to be picked up just anywhere. That's a lot of money these days."

Matt shrugged. "I'm leaving all that, Newt. You'll have at least fifty thousand dollars riding that stage, and *that's* a lot of money."

"We'll advertise, Matt. We'll tell them you're riding shotgun. That should stop them."

"It will stop some of them. It won't stop Harry Meadows."

Clyde almost dropped his cup. "*Meadows?* Is Harry Meadows *here?*".

"He's here. He's holed up over in the Schell Creek Mountains. I picked up his sign yesterday. I found one of his camps in the Fortifications . . . I know his camps. I've followed him long enough. Then I trailed him over to Dutch John."

"But how could he know about the shipment?" Felton asked.

"There's no keeping such a thing secret, Dick. Everybody knows you've struck it rich, everybody knows no ore has been shipped, and they know some at least has been high-grade. You can be sure that anything worth knowing is known to Harry Meadows."

"I never heard of him."

"Wells Fargo has," Clyde replied. "He held up at least five of our stages on the Black Canyon run down in Arizona. He stopped one last year near Sand Springs that cost us a pretty penny. He's known to have operated in Oregon, California, and Colorado, but just as we start to move against him he disappears. He's as wily as a lobo wolf, and he can smell a trap ten miles off."

Laurie Shannon watched the men curiously. She was a girl who listened well, and in the West listening could

be the price of survival. She knew about Newton Clyde
. . . he had the reputation of being one of Wells Fargo's
best men, and had survived a few gun battles himself.

"It isn't only the stage job, Matt," Clyde said. "We
want you to take on the marshal's job over in Confusion."

"No. No to both jobs."

"Matt, think about it. They're running wild over there.
It's going to be a tougher camp than Bodie, tougher than
Pioche or Alta. There's nobody else can handle it."

"No."

"Gentlemen," Laurie interrupted, "it's time for supper.
I take it that none of you is going to refuse my hospital-
ity?"

The kitchen door opened and Joss Ringgold came in
followed by Free Dorset. Clyde recognized Joss, and
grinned at him. "How are you, Joss? It's been a long
time."

Joss grinned back at him. "It'll be longer, Clyde. Much
longer."

Only Coburn smiled. Dorset looked puzzled. "What's
all that about?" he demanded.

"Old joke," Clyde said, brushing it off, "just between
Joss an' me."

They talked quietly, while Laurie put dishes on the
table, and a Mexican girl who appeared as if by magic
from the back of the house brought dishes to the table.
Beef, chili, string beans, and a huge platter heaped with
doughnuts.

"What about Burke?" Clyde said then. "You want him
to ride with somebody else when Harry Meadows is
around?"

Matt looked up, and Laurie, watching with curious,
appraising eyes caught a flash of worry on his face. "I
had forgotten," he said. "I'll take the job."

"And I'll up the ante," Clyde said. "I'll pay you a
hundred for the trip."

"A *hundred* dollars?" Dorset exclaimed. "For *one* trip
to Carson? I'll do it for fifty!"

Clyde glanced at Matt, while Felton watched curiously. It was Ringgold who spoke. "Free, you talk too much. They wouldn't give you fifty, nor twenty-five even. They aren't hirin' a gun, they're hirin' a *man*. They're hirin' judgment, an' the kind of experience you only get the hard way."

Dorset was angry. "A lot you'd know about it, you old fossil!"

"*Free!*" Laurie spoke sharply. "We will have none of that! If you can't be polite, I will ask you to leave."

Dorset was about to speak, but changed his mind and sat down abruptly.

"While we are talking," Newton Clyde said in a slow, conversational tone, "we might bring up the fact that there are few men anywhere who would like to try conclusions with Joss Ringgold with a gun." Dorset looked up, astonished and unbelieving, as Clyde turned to Joss. "Do you mind, Ring? Can I tell them?"

"Matt knows," Ringgold replied, "and so does the boss. So go ahead."

"Fifteen years ago Joss Ringgold was one of the most widely known outlaws in the country. He held up more stages than most of us will ever see. More than anybody, even more than Harry Meadows. He slipped, we caught him, and he did time in Yuma. A few years ago he was pardoned, and I was one of those who circulated a petition asking for that pardon. I think every employee of Wells Fargo signed it.

"Do you know why they signed it? Joss had robbed one of our stages of six thousand in gold and was making a clean getaway when the Apaches attacked the stage he had just left. They wounded the driver and killed the messenger, and then Joss rode back and fought them off until help came."

Freeman Dorset stared at Joss, then sat back in his chair, his mouth shut tight. Occasionally he glanced from one man to the other, still uncertain as to whether he should believe the story or not.

Dorset had hired on at the ranch, very condescending

about working as a plain cowhand, and he had been arrogant about his own skill with a gun. He remembered it now, and felt his cheeks flushing just to think of some of the bragging he had done. Joss had seemed like any old saddle tramp who had never been anything else. It was hard to imagine that the old man he had treated with such casualness had been a noted outlaw.

When the conversation became general, Dorset slipped outside. The air was clear and cold off the mountain, and he stood there thinking, feeling his irritation grow.

That old man? He didn't believe it, not for a minute. No tough man acted like that, so they had to be joshing him, trying to make a fool of him. He'd show them! And then the thought came.... What was that outlaw's name? Harry Meadows?

CHAPTER 6

The next day the type was large across the face of the local newspaper, *The Voice of Confusion*:

CONFUSION SHIPS $50,000 IN GOLD!!

At daybreak tomorrow the mines of Confusion will make their first shipment of gold bullion to Carson City. The gold, largely from the Discovery group, represents the first recovery from the mines of the district.

Matt Coburn will ride shotgun.

The town boosters were elated. This would show all those doubters in Virginia City, San Francisco, and points between that Confusion was no empty boom town, as many had claimed. Also, it would increase the flow of would-be miners into the district, a bonanza for the merchants, the gamblers, the saloon-keepers.

"Damn fools," a stranger muttered, "advertisin' that way! Lettin' every would-be road agent in the Territory know just when the gold is shipped."

"They done it a-purpose," an old-timer said to him sourly. "No road agent in his right mind is goin' to tackle that stage with Matt Coburn a-settin' on the box."

Nobody had seen Matt. He was not in Confusion, nor

was he at the Rafter LS. He was, in fact, lying up in the hills, where he could watch the trails from Confusion to the Fortifications and points west. He had a comfortable spot, a canteen of water, and lunch wrapped in a newspaper. It had been typical of Laurie Shannon that when he asked for the lunch she asked no questions.

The sun was warm and he had been dozing slightly when some minor noise natural to his surroundings caused his eyes to open. All was quiet around him, but far down the length of Spring Valley he could see a tiny cloud of dust and the black speck that meant a horseman. His glasses were strong but the rider was too far away to be identified. Matt watched for several minutes, speculating on that rider.

Harry Meadows had ridden in that direction. So far as Coburn was aware, there was no one else off there, and the speed of this rider implied a definite destination and the necessity for quick arrival.

If the rider was not going to see Meadows, he was of no importance to Coburn. But if he was riding to see him, it must be to tell him of the gold shipment and the fact that Matt was to ride shotgun. So the way to look at it was to take it for granted that he was heading for Meadows' camp.

The question was, who was the rider, and where had he come from? It was not yet ten o'clock in the morning. The *Voice* was not due on the street for another hour or two at the earliest. Newton Clyde would not say anything about Matt's plans, and Felton was neither a talkative man nor a mixer. Anyway, there had not been time for the news to spread, nor for a rider to come this far.

Moreover, no one from Confusion would have a horse still capable of that speed after the long ride from town. Either the rider had gotten a fresh horse from the Rafter LS, or he had started from there.

After a while, Matt Coburn ate his lunch. He had not lived as long as he had without realizing the fallacy of jumping to conclusions. He ate slowly, chewing each bite with appreciation for the flavor of the beef and bread, the taste of the doughnuts. Then he washed it down with water from his canteen.

Finally he got up, tightened the cinch on the appaloosa, checked his rifle, and replaced it in the scabbard. He had never wished to ride shotgun or run a tough town again, but it was the mention of Dandy Burke that had won him over.

Four years before, near Frenchman's Station, Harry Meadows, his brother Archie, and two others had attempted to stop a stage driven by Burke. They had killed the shotgun messenger at the first fire, and Burke had caught up the shotgun and had let Archie Meadows take both barrels in the chest. Then he had escaped with the coach. Harry Meadows had sworn to get Burke, but everybody who knew Harry Meadows at all knew he would not do it until the time was right. To really get Burke you had to take his coach away from him, and then kill him.

It was dusk when Matt Coburn rode into Confusion. He did not ride through the town, but came in over the ridge and went first to Newton Clyde's office. Fife was there, as well as Felton.

"Hello, Sturd." Coburn held out his hand to the newspaper publisher. "Nobody's killed you yet, I see."

"Nor you." Fife handed him a copy of the sheet announcing the stage run. "I gave you some good billing. Right at the top of the sheet."

"Thanks," Matt said dryly. "I didn't need that."

"It was my idea," Clyde said. "I figured it might scare off the small fry."

"It won't scare Meadows, and he knows. He had the word before noon today."

They looked at each other. "How could that be?" Felton asked. "The paper wasn't on the street until nearly two this afternoon."

"He knows." Coburn explained about the rider he had seen, and his own reasoning.

"Joss?" Clyde was incredulous. "You mean he's gone back?"

"I called no names, nor will I." Coburn was emphatic. "I have no idea who was at the Rafter last night, or who rode out of there this morning. I only know that Meadows knows, if he wants to do something about it."

"Do you thnk he will? Isn't he afraid of you?"

Coburn smiled without humor. "He's not afraid of me, or of anybody, but Harry Meadows is a careful man. I don't think he will buck the odds. There will be other gold shipments. Sure, he wants Dandy's scalp, and he wants fifty thousand dollars, but there will be other times when Dandy is less ready and when I am not riding shotgun."

"How about the marshal's job?" Clyde asked.

"No. I'll take your shipment to Carson, and that's the end of it. I'm going to buy some cattle and start my own outfit."

Newton Clyde had taken space in a building put up by Gage, using it for both office and living quarters, and he suggested now, "I have a spare cot, Matt, if you want to bed down there. I'd feel safer. The gold is on the premises."

"All right," Matt said.

When he left the meeting Matt walked out into the street. Removing his hat, he wiped the hatband, thinking as he did so that all these towns sounded alike, and they were alike. He knew what was happening down there now, knew what would happen in the hours to come. Even the faces were the same, although some of the names had changed; the cast was an old one, and familiar to him. He had been a part of that cast too many times; he had walked just such streets as these, sometimes as the law, sometimes as a drifter.

He was a different man now, less patient than he had been, and that was a danger both to himself and to others. Once such towns had been a challenge. He had come into them to bring law and order, but too many of them had only imagined that was what they wanted, and all too often he had discovered that even those who hired him became his enemies. They wanted the money that would be spent, without the turbulence that came with it. The buffalo hunters, the cattle drivers, the prospectors, and the miners were free spenders, but they accompanied their spending with the release of exuberant spirits that started with shouts and raucous laughter and too much whiskey, and often ended in gunfire.

Fife came out to stand beside him. For a minute or two neither man spoke, and then it was Fife who said, "She's a doozer, Matt, she's a rip-snortin' doozer! There's eight to ten ready killers down there, and twice that many murderers, and on top of that there's the lads who like it rough. You'll find a lot of old friends down there."

"Not many, Sturd. A man in my line of work doesn't have too many friends."

"You *should* have friends. You've made a dozen towns decent to live in."

"But not for their kind. They like them rough, Sturd. I used to think I did."

The stars were out. Up at Discovery there were lights. Felton and his partners were working a night shift. The Treasure Vault was also working, and there were a couple of men busy at the Slum Bucket.

"Nathan Bly's down there, Matt. He killed a man a couple of days ago who'd accused him of cheating."

"He asked for it, then. Nathan Bly never cheated anybody."

"He's fast, Matt. Quicker on the shoot then he used to be, and he doesn't go as far with them."

So Bly was losing his patience, too? Was it that, or had they both become killers? Had they, somewhere along the line, lost their perspective? Had the ability to kill become a willingness to kill?

"What about Thompson?" he asked.

"Ah, now. There's a bad one, Matt. He's mean, he's vicious and low-down. But he's fast. He drinks a lot, but he shoots just as straight when he's drunk. And many a time he acts the drunk when he's cold sober. He likes it, Matt. He makes his brag that the man doesn't live who can stand face to face to him with either fists or guns. I'd say he weighs about two hundred and sixty, and not over five to ten pounds of it blubber. Over at Eureka he smashed Tim Sullivan down, then put the boots to him. Crippled him for life.

"He made his reputation whipping loggers up in Oregon. He was a river man until he found he could live easier with a fist and a gun. They say he's killed twenty men. Cut that in half, if you're talking gun or knife battles, but he killed one man with his fists.

"And Peggoty Gorman is almost as bad. He's a sandbagger or a knife man, does his work in an alley. He used to be an acrobat in the old country, but they shipped him out for murder."

Leaving Fife chewing on the stub of a cigar and listening to the town, Matt went into Clyde's quarters and pulled off his boots, then hung up his gunbelt, the butt of his gun close at hand.

The last thing he remembered was the muttering of some drunken miners as they wandered past the building. Clyde was already asleep.

It was cold and dark when he awoke. He lay perfectly still for a few minutes. The town was quiet. There were no sounds in the room except for the breathing of the Wells Fargo man. Matt struck a match, and shielding it with his hand, glanced at his watch. It lacked a few minutes of five o'clock.

He swung his feet to the floor, and dressed swiftly and silently. Then he went into the next room, and having lighted the coal-oil lamp, he shaved and combed his hair carefully. Taking his hat, he stepped out into the darkness of predawn.

The stage was already standing in the street and he helped Burke hook up the trace chains.

Dandy Burke was a slender man of thirty-odd. He was smoking the stub of a cigar when he came around the lead team. "Are you ready for this?" he asked.

"Ready as I'll ever be. I could use some coffee, though."

"Come on over. Felton's up, and Dan Cohan just took the pot off the fire."

Four men stood around nursing cups and looking as if sleep was still in them that the coffee had not warmed away.

"Shotgun." Felton pointed.

"I've got my own," Matt said.

Burke picked it up. "I'll take that. I've seen the time I wanted one."

Matt Coburn let his eyes take in the group. Felton, Cohan, Zeller, and Newton Clyde, who had come over while Matt was helping Burke with the team. Clyde was a good man—these Wells Fargo men always were, and they were in every new camp, ready to ship gold before there was even a post office.

Matt's eyes dropped to the cases on the floor. These in addition to the cases across the street? "We'll be carrying more than fifty thousand, then," he said, indicating them.

Felton looked at him. "An even hundred thousand," he said, "if their figures match ours."

Matt took a deep breath. If Harry Meadows knew there was that much he would take the gamble, Matt Coburn or no.

"We hit a pocket," Cohan said. "We lifted one nugget that weighed nine pounds, and we hit some thick seams just loaded with it."

You could not keep a thing like that quiet, and Matt knew it. He saw Dandy Burke's face. The Irishman looked grim.

"I made a bargain," Matt said quietly, "but Dandy ought to have more money."

"He's getting fifty," Felton said somewhat testily.

"Did you ever sit up on that box holding the lines on some half-broke broncs while you're getting shot at? If I'd known there was that much gold I'd never have agreed to the price. Once the story gets out, every thief in the country will be riding."

"All right," Felton agreed reluctantly.

Matt Coburn turned abruptly and went outside. For the first time he was really worried. Fifty thousand was a lot of gold—but twice that much? And the story of the big nugget would surely get out. There was excitement in such a story, and there was challenge.

Dandy Burke came outside. "Thanks," he said. "That was decent of you."

"You've got it coming," Matt said. "You'll earn it."

"Let's have some more coffee."

While they were drinking the coffee Matt saw some people coming up the street—two men and a woman. The woman was not with the men, but walked slightly behind them.

Holding the cup in his hands, he watched them. The men were strangers. One was a stocky, wide-shouldered, bearded man with quick movements and a tough, capable look about him. The other man was slender, better dressed, but not a gambler, Matt decided, and probably not a businessman.

The woman was scarcely more than a girl, young but with no wide-eyed innocence about her. She was dressed very well for the time and place, and wore no make-up. She carried only a carpetbag.

Newton Clyde came out, followed by Cohan and Felton. "Passengers?" Matt inquired quietly, over his cup.

"There will be four," Clyde said. "Matt Coburn, meet Charlie Kearns"—this was the stocky, bearded man—"and Peter Dunning."

The girl had halted, well behind the others, but Clyde made no move to introduce her until the two men had acknowledged the introductions and gone inside for coffee.

"Matt," Clyde said quietly, "this is Madge Healy."

The girl's eyes were on his face, awaiting a reaction, but Matt's smile was casual and friendly. "Howdy, ma'am." He held his hat in his hand. "I hope you won't mind a rough ride."

Her chin lifted slightly and she looked straight into his

eyes. "I have had some rough rides, Mr. Coburn. I think I can stay with you."

"You know," he said gently, "I think you could, at that. Would you like some coffee?"

"Yes, please.'

He went inside and took a clean cup from the shelf. The men were standing about, most of them silent. It was a cold morning, they had only just gotten out of bed, and they did not feel talkative.

He took the coffee outside. "It's hot," he warned. "Be careful."

"Thank you."

He put his hat on and stood beside her as she sipped the coffee. "If there is anything you want," he said, "just tap on the underside of the roof. I'll hear you."

"I will be all right." She hesitated ever so little, and then said, "Mr. Coburn, you are a gentleman."

He made no reply, and she looked up to see his eyes were on the man who was walking up the street. The fourth passenger.

He was a lean, wiry man wearing a black coat and a tied-down gun. He carried a blanket roll in his left hand, which he tossed to the stage-top. Only then did he turn to face them, looking first at Matt, then at Madge Healy.

He had deep, sunken eyes, and thin brows on a narrow face. When he looked at Matt, the gaze straight but the eyes curiously unalive, Matt was reminded of a snake he had once seen at close quarters. The man's clothing was new, a store-bought outfit still showing the creases of the packing case. Only the gun was not new. It was a gun that showed much use.

"You drivin'?" he asked.

"No, Dandy Burke is driving. He's inside right now."

The man turned away, and when he had gone inside the girl said, "Do you know him?"

"No."

"That is Pike Sides, the Cherry Creek gunman."

"Thanks."

Matt knew something about him. He was from West

Virginia by way of Texas and Old Mexico. He had killed a man in Chihuahua, another in Durango. He had been involved briefly in the Lincoln County War, had been involved in a shooting in Veral, Utah, and had killed a man in Pioche and another at Silver Reef. He was occasionaly a gambler, and his gun was for hire.

Burke came out and lit the lamp on the near side of the coach.

"I wouldn't do that, Dandy," Matt said quietly. "Anyway, it will be light soon."

Kearns and Dunning emerged from the shack and mounted the step to the coach. Matt helped Madge Healy in, then stepped to the door and took his shotgun from under his slicker. He carried the slicker out, too, holding under it a gunbelt loaded with shotgun shells.

Pike Sides came out, glancing from the shotgun to Matt Coburn. "You the ol' bull o' the woods around here?" he asked.

"Just a hired hand," Matt replied carelessly. "If I hold this shotgun while I ride they give me a free trip."

Sides grinned, but said nothing and mounted to the stage. Dandy Burke glanced at Clyde. "All right, boys. Let her go."

Burke swung up and Matt Coburn followed. Matt looked down at the little crowd around the shack that doubled as a stage station—Felton, Cohan and Zeller, Buckwalter, Gage, Clyde. He lifted a hand and Burke cracked his whip and the horses leaned into the harness.

The stage went down the rocky street, swung into the trail, and headed for the main trail at Cowboy Pass. Matt held his shotgun between his knees and lighted a cigar.

"You think Madge is leaving?" Burke asked. "Is she pulling her freight?"

Matt considered the question, then shook his head. "I doubt it. She's held on for a while, and she's game. Game as they come."

"You think she did it?"

"No. But I wouldn't have blamed her."

"He was a skunk."

Dandy Burke popped his whip over the heads of the leaders and the team straightened out to run. They swung into Cowboy Pass just where it emerged into Snake Valley. The land opened wide before them, the trail showing across the dusty plain toward the far-off, towering mountains of the Snake Range.

As the team lined out on the trail, Matt pointed ahead. "Stay with it, Dandy. Don't make the turn."

"The best trail is south of here."

"I know it. The trail west is good enough when it's dry, and it's dry now. I scouted it a few days ago."

Matt Coburn rolled his cigar into the corner of his mouth and, still holding the shotgun between his knees, he could reach the belt of shotgun shells around his waist under his coat. He had a handful of shells bulging each pocket. They were for Indians, like the rifle at his feet. With outlaws it was one or two shots as a rule, and he had them or they had him. So far they had never had him.

Dust devils danced on the valley floor. Over there near Jeff Davis Peak was Sacremento Pass, tallest peak in the range. The pass was the first danger, now that they had avoided skirting the hills to the south.

"Take it fast across the valley, ease up at the foot of the mountains. We're going to change horses at Silver Creek."

Burke glanced at him. "They'll be expecting us at the station."

"I know it."

The team was a good one. He had six head of broncs, half broken but full of guts and ready to run their hearts out.

Matt Coburn turned and looked back the way they had come, then let his eyes turn toward the main trail, the way they should have come. There was no dust yet.

You had to give them time. He knew they would be coming soon.

CHAPTER 7

Freeman Dorset was frightened. It was a feeling he would have admitted to no one, not even to himself. He had acted, as always, on an impulse.

He considered himself a dangerous man. He was a good shot, and he carried himself with a good deal of dash and swagger. He had practiced with a gun until he was fast—exceptionally fast, he believed.

Wherever he went, when there was talk of gun-fighters and gunmen it was Hickok, Courtright, Wes Harden, and Billy the Kid who were talked of. But among those who knew the mining-camp country there was more talk of Langford Peel, John Bull, Jim Levy, Calvin Bell, or Matt Coburn. Always, always, Matt Coburn.

Dorset had taken the job riding for Rafter reluctantly. It was beneath him to be just a rider, earning thirty dollars a month. He was a gun-hand, a gun for hire. When he realized that Coburn was to get a hundred dollars for riding to Carson City, he was astounded.

His own offer, made suddenly, without thinking, had been simply ignored. Then, to top it all, Joss Ringgold, whom he had treated contemptuously as an old cowhand, proved to have been an outlaw with a reputa-

58

tion. The old man had probably been laughing at him all the time. Dorset's cheeks burned at the thought.

At the mention of Harry Meadows, who was not afraid of Coburn, Dorset suddenly made up his mind. He would show them who was afraid of Matt Coburn!

Coburn had mentioned following Meadows, and instantly Free Dorset knew where Meadows had gone. More than two weeks before, hunting strays and checking available grass and water, Dorset had sighted a thin rise of smoke. Curious, he investigated. A lone man was camped in a tiny park, and from the appearance of the camp he had been there for some time. Later, checking again, he had seen two men in the camp. Without doubt, it was there Meadows was hiding.

At first it was only the idea that had just come to him. It was like many of those other times when he had vowed to himself that he would show somebody— something he had in his mind but had no serious thought of doing. But in this case he had done it—he had ridden to Meadows' camp.

There were four men in the camp when he rode down the dim trail into the park. There were eight horses, but only four saddles and two packsaddles. He kept himself well in the open and came down the trail with no attempt at concealment.

Three of the men were about his own age, or a year or two older. One of them was a lean, dark, savage-looking man with long hair and a tied-down gun. "Are you Meadows?" he asked.

The somewhat older man who was seated on the ground with his back to a log spoke up. He had thin blond hair, a sparse beard—in general a nondescript appearance. "I'm Meadows. Who are you?"

"I'm Freeman Dorset. I came huntin' Harry Meadows because I heard he wasn't afraid of Matt Coburn."

Meadows sat up slowly, his eyes on Dorset. "Now, where did you hear a thing like that?"

"Matt Coburn said it himself. They were talkin' how

somebody might hold up the stage when it leaves Confusion with the gold."

"Coburn said that, did he? What else did he say?"

"He didn't figure you'd try it. He said you were too smart. Said there'd be other times when he wasn't riding shotgun."

Harry Meadows chewed thoughtfully on a blade of grass. After a moment he said, "Where was this? And who was there?"

"At the Rafter. I'm workin' over there while I size things up. This here seemed to me to be a good thing if I had the right people with me."

"I asked who else was there."

"Newt Clyde, that Wells Fargo gent, Dick Felton from the Discovery mines at Confusion, and my boss. She's Laurie Shannon."

Meadows chewed on the grass blade in silence. Dorset found himself growing impatient. "They'll be carrying fifty thousand in gold," he said with authority. "That's enough for all of us."

Nobody commented for a minute or two, then one of the others spoke up. "What I want to know is what Coburn was doin' at the Rafter?"

Meadows took the grass from his teeth. "Is he ridin' a appaloosy—black an' white?"

"Uh-huh—a good horse, too."

"So ... we might have knowed. You figure that was him, Kendrick?"

"Who else? I told you somebody was skirtin' around the hills kind of aimless-like ... like he had nowheres to go and plenty of time to get there. You think he's spotted us, Harry?"

"Look at it," Harry Meadows said. "Even this greenhorn had us spotted. I should have figured on that, on'y it didn't seem likely anybody would be around these hills."

"He's just one man," Dorset interrupted. "He's got just two hands."

They ignored him. He stared at them angrily. What

had he come over here for, anyway? As he shaped the question his mind suddenly asked him: Well, why *had* he come?

Was he aiming to turn outlaw? Or was it simply that he was jealous of Matt Coburn's reputation? Was it because he himself had no reputation?

"I want in," he said sharply. "After all, I told you about Coburn and the fifty thousand."

"We knew about Coburn," Kendrick said roughly. "We've known for days. We knew he was going to be asked before it ever happened."

"And the shipment won't be fifty thousand, it will be a hundred thousand," Harry Meadows said, "but who wants to buy the kind of trouble Matt Coburn has to offer?"

"We'd have to kill him," one of the men said, "else he'd follow us to hell an' gone."

Harry Meadows was wary of a trap. Like an old plains coyote, he was as shrewd as he was dangerous. His career as an outlaw had been uniformly successful in evading the law, even if he had not always come off with the big strikes.

He had grown up in the back country of Missouri, one of a family who had lived off well-to-do people on the flatlands, stealing stock, occasionally raiding country stores. Then as a boy he had struck out for the West, selling liquor to Indians, stealing cattle and horses, and finally stealing money.

Wells Fargo had occasion to know him well. He was not a man to be lured by big money, for big money incurred big risks, and Harry Meadows had been born without a reckless bone in his tough, wiry body. He liked living and he liked his freedom, and his strikes had been carefully planned, neatly executed, with no false motion.

The one man whom he had reason to hate was Dandy Burke. There had been $9,000 in the Wells Fargo box, and Meadows knew it. He had stopped the stage near the crest of a steep grade and ordered Burke to get down. As Burke got down he spoke to his team, and

well-trained as they were, they commenced to back up.
Meadows, who had not heard Burke's low-voiced command, was irritated by this. The edge of the trail was
too close and it was six hundred feet to the bottom of
the canyon. "Stop them!" he ordered.

Dandy Burke obligingly climbed back on the box,
took up the reins, and said over his shoulder something
about "... on top." He eased the stage forward, and as it
topped the ridge Dandy let go a wild Texas yell,
cracked his whip over the leaders, and the stage lunged
ahead, leaving Harry Meadows standing with his mouth
open as it raced around a bend and out of sight.

The story had been told and laughed at in every bar
and bunkhouse over half a dozen states, and Harry
Meadows did not like being laughed at. He had made
known his displeasure, and had voiced his intentions
toward Burke, when and if he found him again.

Now he was faced with a problem. He wanted Burke,
and he wanted the hundred thousand. His spies in Confusion had reported the find of the nugget and had told
how large the shipment would actually be, but Meadows
wanted no part of Matt Coburn.

Now he thought he saw a way.

He glanced up at Dorset, and gestured to his gun. "Are
you any good with that?"

"You're damn right I am!"

"As good as Coburn?"

"Well," Dorset said with elaborate carelessness, "I've
heard a lot of talk, but I never seen any of his graveyards."

Kendrick caught a glimmering of what Meadows had
in mind, and said, "Nobody could be blamin' you if you
was afraid to tackle him."

"Who said I was afraid?" Dorset demanded.

"He's not scared." Meadows sat up. "I can size 'em up,
Kendrick. Dorset ain't scared. Anyway, why should he
be? Coburn is mostly reputation. He isn't all that fast."

Meadows started to roll a cigarette. "Anyway, Dorset
wants to join up with us ... at least for this deal. Now,

we already knew about the shipment and how big it was, an' he's smart enough to know if we want that gold we've got just one problem."

Harry Meadows touched his tongue to the paper. "I think Dorset is just the man for it. He's fast with a gun, he ain't one least bit scared of Matt Coburn, so he's just the man to stop him."

"To what?" Freeman Dorset had an uncomfortable feeling that things were moving faster than he wanted, and in a direction he had not considered.

"To stop Coburn. To put a bullet into him."

"Man, what a scalp that would be!" Kendrick agreed. "To be known as the man who downed Matt Coburn!"

"Now, just a minute!" Dorset protested. "I ain't the least bit scared of Matt Coburn, but I—"

"Strawberry Station, that would be the place," Meadows interrupted. "Dorset could make his own plans. He'll know best how it should be done, but it ought to be at Strawberry, right at the opening of Sacramento Pass through the Snakes. If Dorset puts Coburn out of action at Strawberry, we could take the stage in the pass. A thing like that, gettin' rid of Coburn, that would call for a big slice of the pie—maybe twenty-five thousand of it."

The others looked at Harry Meadows, but he avoided their eyes. "Up on the box, with that shotgun, Coburn could be mighty hard to handle, but down on the ground at Strawberry, unexpected-like . . ."

"Now, wait just a minute!" Dorset protested again.

The dark, savage-looking man spoke up. "For that much," he said, "I'll tackle him myself."

Meadows shook his head. "He knows Dorset here. He could get close to him, take him unexpected-like . . . not that he'd need to, y'understand."

"Twenty-five thousand dollars!" Kendrick said, drawing a long breath. "That's a sight of money."

Freeman Dorset was perplexed. How had he gotten into this situation anyway? He had come here in anger and some spite, only half in the notion of doing anything about it, and now instead of perhaps having a hand in a stage holdup, here he was being saddled with a shooting, and of Matt Coburn, of all people.

"You can see he's not the kind to scare easy," Meadows persisted. "Coburn probably takes him for nothing but a loose-mouthed kid. Wait'll he sees him with a gun in his hand!"

To back out would seem cowardly, but Dorset wanted desperately to back out. He was not conscious of any fear of Matt Coburn, it was simply that he had not bargained for any of this. What he had done had been done on the impulse of a moment, but getting in was easier than getting out.

"I'll have to think about it," he said lamely. "I'd need to plan, see how it shapes up."

"Nothing to plan," Meadows persisted, "nothing to shape up. Coburn will ride the stage into Strawberry. He'll find everything as it should be. He'll be tired, off-guard. How you do it is your own affair, but it'll be dark, and I'd say the best thing is to suddenly yell at him. 'Who's a liar?' an' shoot as you yell. He'll be dead, and folks will say he called you a liar and you beat him to the draw."

Free Dorset was a weak young man, and he was tempted. He had seen the awe that surrounded men like Matt Coburn; he had seen the way heads turned when they passed, and how strong men moved aside for them. He was torn between what he wanted and the sneaking realization that he was not man enough to bring it off. Yet that realization was only a dark shadow in the back of his mind, and he could already see himself walking hard-booted down the boardwalks of western towns, pointed out as "the man who killed Matt Coburn." He had dreamed of such a thing, and now the possibility was here.

Along with it, twenty-five thousand dollars in gold. More than he was likely to see in a lifetime of hard work.

"I don't need no tricks. I can beat him without them."

"Sure you can. But why not a little insurance?"

"If you'd leave right now," Kendrick suggested, "you could be there waitin' when the stage pulled in."

"I wasn't figurin' on anything like this," Dorset protested. "I mean, bein' gone so long. Miss Shannon, she's sure to be wonderin' whatever happened."

"Don't let that worry you none a-tall," Meadows replied easily. "You just ride over to the Rafter. Before evenin' one o' the boys will come driftin' by an' say how he seen some Rafter stock over next to Strawberry. She's o'ny got you an' that ol' man, an' he won't be beggin' for no ride. If she don't ask you to go, you just speak up and offer, but give her a chance to ask."

Harry Meadows smiled. "That will put you in Strawberry in time. You take care of Coburn an' we'll take care of the stage, an' you'll get your piece right off."

That was the way they left it. Before sundown it was Scarff the dark, hard-faced young man who rode up to the ranch.

"Light an sit," Laurie said. "It's hash-time."

"Got to make Confusion t'night. Got some mail for Fife an' Buckwalter." He glanced at the brands on the horses, indicating them. "Seen some stock o' yours clean over by Sacramento Pass ... just this side of Strawb'ry. Seems a far piece."

"*Rafter* stock?" Laurie Shannon stared. "How many head?"

"I on'y seen eight or nine brands ... there was about fifteen in the bunch, though."

Scarff hung up the dipper and swung to the saddle. "Got to be ridin', ma'am. Thanks for the water."

Joss Ringgold came up from the stable as the rider was leaving. "Who was that?" he asked.

Laurie explained, and Joss was obviously puzzled. Dorset strolled up and stood listening. "Seems odd," Ringgold commented. "Water's good here, and so's the grass."

"Do you suppose that old blue cow would try to go

home? I bought thirty or forty head from Steptoe Valley."

"No accountin' for critters," Joss said thoughtfully. "That man was ridin' a mighty fine horse for a cowhand," he added.

"He's carryin' mail for Confusion. At least for Fife and Buckwalter. He would need a good horse for that."

Laurie turned on Dorset. "Free, how would you like to take a ride? Bring that stock back from Strawberry? You could spend the night there and start back the next day."

"All right. Sure." Free turned away quickly, then stopped. He seemed about to speak, then walked on without saying anything.

Joss Ringgold watched him go frowning a little, but he made no comment.

Neither did Laurie Shannon, but when a girl has lived most of her life among riding men and stock, she notices things. Something was disturbing her, but she could not decide exactly what it was. Several times during the evening she caught herself pausing in whatever she was doing, and looking off into space with a frown on her face.

It was not until she awoke the following morning that it came to her, and at first she could make nothing of it.

CHAPTER 8

Matt Coburn did not believe that it was when his time came that he would die. With the harsh realism that was typical of him, he believed he would cash in his chips whenever he became careless.

He was always aware that speed and accuracy were not enough, for one had to live with the kind of awareness a wild creature develops, sensitive to every change of shadow, every alteration of mood in those about him. His natural liking for his fellowman was tempered by a cynical knowledge that all men were liable to temptation.

Now he turned again to glance at the back trail, but still there was no dust, and the fact worried him.

His thoughts reached ahead, searching out every mile of the trail, considering the most obviously dangerous spots, and those which were potentially dangerous. Knowing that Harry Meadows was in the area was reason enough to expect the unexpected, for the man had a foxlike cunning as well as a vanity as easily offended as a woman's. And Dandy Burke had outwitted him, left him standing in the road while the stage disappeared around a curve.

Strawberry was a possibility, but by changing teams at Silver Creek Ranch he could bypass the stage station

and gain several minutes on his time. His big silver
watch told him that Dandy was already running a good
five minutes ahead of schedule.

If an attempt was planned for the pass, they would be
waiting either just before the crest of the ridge or near
the bottom of the pass. The latter would be typical of
Meadows—to hit them just when they were breathing a
sigh of relief at escaping trouble.

Beyond, there was a wide-open stretch which was
relatively safe, and then came Connors' Pass.

The Silver Creek ranch house was a long, low-roofed
building with three doors opening into the ranch yard.
One end of the house was the bunkhouse, the center
was the kitchen and dining room, and the other end
housed the family. The house was built of logs with
loopholes for defense. In every direction there was a
good field of fire.

There were several corrals, and Drumright always
kept stock ready for use. He employed half a dozen
hands on the premises, and his place had been a stopping point for travelers long before the stage line had
started operation.

Through his field glasses, Matt Coburn surveyed the
ranch with care before he approached it. Drawn up for
a breather on top of a small knoll, he took his time
studying the layout to see that all was as usual. A few
minutes later they wheeled into the yard, and Matt
dropped to the ground. Drumright and two of his hands
had come out to meet them.

"Hank, can you give us a team?" Matt asked. "And give
my people some coffee and sandwiches right now?"

Drumright was not a man who asked questions. If
Matt Coburn was riding shotgun there was a reason for
it. He turned swiftly, "Joe ... Pete ... get that brown
team out. I want them under harness in ten minutes!"

He turned to the passengers who were stepping down.
"Go on in," he said. "There's always something ready at
Drumright's."

Charlie Kearns and Peter Dunning were crossing the

yard toward the house when Matt helped Madge Healy down.

Hank Drumright turned sharply, his hard eyes taking her in at a glance. He started to speak, but Coburn was first. Matt had seen it coming, and headed it off. "Miss Healy is going to Carson with us, Hank. She'll be coming back on the next stage. Sturd Fife an' Newt Clyde were down to see her off."

Hank looked at him, closed his mouth, and strode over to the corral.

Madge hesitated beside Matt, holding her skirt free of the dust with one hand. "You needn't have said that, Matt. I can fight my own battles." And then she added, "I always have, I guess."

Matt grinned at her. "Forget it, Madge. Newt and Sturd won't mind, and you'll have to admit they were down at the stage when you left. Besides, there's no two men in this country that Hank Drumright respects more."

Pike Sides had moved up beside Matt, and now he said, "We aren't stopping at Strawberry? Is that the idea?"

"That's the idea."

It was smooth and fast, as Matt had known it would be. He stood at one side, shotgun in hand, back to the wall and watching everything, a cup of coffee in his left hand.

Hank Drumright prided himself on being prepared for any emergency, and always had. You paid, but you got the service you asked for, promptly and without questions. Newt Clyde had commented once that Drumright could have and would have outfitted a war party of Indians if they had ridden up with the money to pay for it.

Madge was the first one outside, walking quickly to the coach. Kearns followed, watching her get into the coach. Peter Dunning came up more slowly and paused near Matt. "Is it true what they say about her?" Dunning asked.

Matt glanced at him, his eyes cold. "Mr. Dunning, you look like a gentleman. I expect that you are."

Dunning flushed and started to speak, but Matt had walked away. He was standing off to one side, midway between the coach and the ranch house, when Pike Sides came out.

Pike hesitated, looking at the open space between himself and the coach, then at Matt Coburn. Deliberately, he took out a cigarette and lighted it, then he walked to the coach without another glance at Matt.

On the box when the stage was rolling, Dandy asked, "What was all that about?"

"Being careful. Pike Sides never rode a stage in his life unless there was a reason for it."

"You think he's goin' to try his luck?"

After a moment's consideration, Matt shook his head. "No. It's something else. There's too much going on, Dandy. I don't know what it is. I can't even guess why Madge is on the coach."

Burke took the stage around a huge pile of boulders while Matt held his shotgun up in his hands, eyes alert for movement. They stretched out on the trail with a straight two miles of open country before them. Matt let his eyes check the sides of the trail ... he did not trust even the empty land.

"She's packin' a gun," Burke said suddenly. "I saw it when she opened her bag at Drumright's."

Matt Corburn looked at him, his mind turning over the information, considering it. Why Madge's sudden trip? Why the gun? Was she carrying it for herself? Or for somebody else? Somebody who might want to use it suddenly?

He had known of Madge Healy for several years. She was an unusually attractive girl, in a country where girls of any kind had been few. She had come to Eureka as only a child, with a traveling show, and she had left the show there with her aunt and her aunt's lover.

For several months they had toured the mining camps, with Madge singing, dancing, and doing monologues for the miners, who had loved her and responded richly. During all those months neither Madge's aunt nor her lover had done anything, living well off Madge's earnings, and then one night while both lay in a drunken sleep, Madge bought a horse and rode out of town.

In Austin she hired the widow of an Irish miner and an old Negro who drove the rig for them and played a banjo. Madge had been fourteen at the time, prematurely wise, prematurely cynical.

Bookings or theatres were no concern of hers. For the next two years she had successfully eluded her aunt and her friend, doing her act wherever a crowd could be assembled, working from loading platforms, piles of lumber, stumps in the woods, in barrooms, cafés, even in livery stables.

She looked younger than she was; she laughed, she was gay, and she sang. She sang the songs the miners remembered from their earlier years. She brought back memories of home, and they loved her for it.

Most of the crowds had money, and they had few places to spend it. They filled the collection hat with coins, bills, nuggets, even small sacks of dust. Every boom camp in Nevada, California, Utah, and Colorado knew her in the next few years. And then suddenly she was no longer a child. She was a young woman, and it was obvious to everyone.

At that moment her aunt's lover finally caught up with her. The aunt, so he said, had died of acute alcoholism, but she had turned over to him papers which made him Madge's legal guardian. He then, as Madge told them in the courtroom later, decided to be her lover as well as her guardian. She refused, and he had moved to use force. And Madge Healy shot him.

She was promptly and enthusiastically acquitted.

Now the atmosphere had changed. No longer a child, she still received applause and money, and proposals as well, and other suggestions of a less permanent nature.

Suddenly and inexplicably, Madge Healy retired, buying a rundown ranch on the edge of Spring Valley, stocking it with a few cattle and some fine horses. Within the year she had gone off to Denver and returned with a husband.

Matt Coburn eased the shotgun on his knees. The trail was closing in. It might be coming up now. This could be the place. Strawberry was right ahead. . . .

With one part of his mind he was still thinking about Madge Healy. He had met her husband, Scollard, only once, in Pioche. He was tall, somewhat sly-looking, but handsome and with polish. He was connected with some banking family in the East, supposedly, and had met Madge through some business arrangement.

He had treated his wife with a kind of lazy contempt, had brought her to town, left her in her hotel room, and spent the biggest part of the night drinking and gambling. While drunk, he had put money on the table, boasting "there's plenty where that came from."

He lost, and lost heavily, and later that night there was a row in the hotel room, and before daybreak somebody reported that Scollard had come slipping down the back stairs, stuffing papers into a valise. He had rented a buckboard and driven swiftly away.

Two days later the buckboard, drawn by two gaunted horses, returned to the livery stable in Pioche. There was a pistol, a derringer known to have belonged to Scollard, lying on the floor of the buckboard near the seat, its butt bloodstained. The derringer carried two loads, one of which had been fired.

When the marshal back-tracked the buckboard he found Scollard. He was dead beside the road, shot twice in the chest. The valise stuffed with papers was gone.

"Didn't you ride out with the posse?" Coburn had asked the marshal later.

"Yeah. The way we figured was that somebody had stopped him, they talked it around a bit, judging by the tracks, and then there was this shooting. It didn't look like a holdup, because whoever killed him had talked to him while he smoked a couple of cigarettes. It looked like Scollard tried a shot and missed ... the other feller didn't."

"Feller?"

"Well," Burke said with a sidewise glance, "there were some who said that Madge shot him. It looked like he was runnin' out on her. His gear was in the buckboard, and it must have been all stowed there before he ever started gambling ... looked like he'd planned on pulling out all the while. Only thing missing was those papers, and at least three people saw him with that valise."

"Was there any evidence against Madge?"

"None whatever. As far's anybody knows, she never left her hotel room. If she did, nobody saw her, or if they did they won't talk. She didn't know anything about it, or any reason why he should be out on the road at that hour, so there it lays."

Coburn cleared his mind of any thought of Madge Healy. Strawberry lay right around the bend.

"Take her right on through, Dandy, at a dead run!" he said.

Burke nodded and, bracing his feet, curled the whip over the heads of the leaders with a crack like a pistol shot. They swept around the bend at a run. Strawberry consisted only of a small stone building with an awning roof, corrals, and a makeshift shed. The stage team was standing out, harnessed and ready.

Matt Coburn was not looking at the team. His eyes swept the yard. He saw the stage tender, the station operator, and another man, a lone cowhand who stood as if waiting for the stage, although his horse stood tied and ready at the rail.

The cowhand, Matt saw, was Freeman Dorset, who rode for Laurie Shannon's Rafter outfit.

There was that fleeting glimpse, and then the stage was gone in a cloud of dust, plunging downgrade into a hollow, then mounting the other side. One more glimpse, and it was gone.

Freeman Dorset stood staring, unable to adjust to the

sudden arrival and disappearance of the stage. He started forward, started to yell, then subsided.

He had been all keyed up for this. He was ready. He had decided to jump Coburn, just as Harry Meadows had suggested. Now Coburn was gone, the stage was gone, and there had been no chance. His first sensation was an overwhelming one, of sheer relief.

"What happened?" he asked. "Why didn't they stop?"

The hostler looked disgusted. "They picked up a team at Silver Creek. I'd know those browns anywhere."

Dorset stared after the coach. All that remained now was the dust settling ... even the sound was gone. This was something Harry Meadows had not foreseen, so what would he do now? What, in fact, would he, Freeman Dorset, do?

Gone were his dreams of fame and adulation, gone all that twenty-five thousand dollars might have bought.

Unless ... suppose, just suppose he could overtake the stage? Suppose he could beat them to the next stop?

No sooner did he think of that than he gave it up. The stage was traveling too fast.

He had missed his chance. He had missed it for now, anyway.

CHAPTER 9

Half a mile beyond Strawberry, Burke slowed his team for the climb up the pass. It was very hot, and the team needed a breather after their hard run. At this point there was small risk, for a cliff rose sheer from the road on one side, and the ground dropped off steeply at the other. To attempt a holdup along this stretch the thieves would have to wait for the coach right in the middle of the road.

"Strawb'ry looked all right," Burke commented.

"Uh-huh." Coburn was wondering about Dorset. He was quite a distance from the home ranch.

Matt thought to himself that it was time he quit this business. He was getting jumpy. The necessity for continual alertness, the suspicion engendered by the work itself, these were changing him. He could feel it, and he did not like it; but he had the reputation and it was the best way he knew how to make a living.

Often he had wondered why others did not quit; now he could see it was not an easy thing to change the pattern of one's life. He could quit and go East, but what could he do there? All he knew was the West, stage lines, freighter outfits, and cattle. Maybe a little about mining. But what they wanted him for was his

75

gun and his knowledge of how and when—above all when—to use it.

At the top of the rise, Burke drew up to let his horses catch their breath, and Pike Sides swung down, standing in the trail, looking forward, then back.

He looked up at Coburn, a curious grin on his face. "The worst of it is ahead," Pike Sides said. "You know that, don't you?"

Matt shrugged. "Maybe." He had dropped to the road beside Pike.

"Whatever happens between here and Carson," Pike said, "you can count me in. I'm riding shotgun, too." The two men walked ahead a little way.

"For yourself?" Matt asked.

"Let's just say I don't want to lose anything." He turned his hard, flat eyes toward Matt. "I'm ridin' herd on more than you. An' more likely to get stopped."

"Are you trying to tell me something? Or just talking?"

"Lettin' you know that you've got another gun. A good one."

"I know it's good," Matt said. "I've seen you work, and if you're riding shotgun on something, that's your business. I'll be glad of the help."

Burke started the coach toward them, walking the team to keep them from stiffening. Matt Coburn stopped where he had a view of the road ahead, but only in glimpses as it curved around among the hills. The trail appeared to be empty. There was no dust.

There would be none, of course. Anybody who wanted this coach would have been planted here hours ago, just waiting. He knew that and Burke knew it, and they only hoped, by moving fast, to come upon them before they were quite set and in position.

The coach drew abreast of the two men and Sides caught at the open door and swung in. Matt noted that he sat facing the rear. Matt swung up, and after a moment he quietly told Burke what Pike Sides had said.

Burke was as puzzled as Matt was. "There's something here," Burke said, "something I don't read."

He walked the team another quarter of a mile and then the downward grade steepened and he started them at a trot.

"No whip, no yells," Matt cautioned, "unless you see them."

"You think it will be Meadows?"

"Maybe ... and if Pike's telling the truth we may get hit twice."

Burke's face grew taut. "I don't like that, Matt. I don't like it at all."

The coach picked up speed. Matt was thinking of the trail ahead. There were a dozen places, at least a dozen, where it might happen.

As they raced down the long hill he was thinking of Dandy Burke. The stage driver accepted the idea that they might be held up, but that they might be stopped twice worried him. It was a matter of the odds, Matt supposed. You could win once or twice, but you could not expect to win them all.

From the top of a ridge a watcher with field glasses had picked up Matt Coburn, and with a mirror he had flashed the signal to Harry Meadows.

"Wrap it up, boys." Meadows said, and walked to his horse. "We're passing this one up."

Scarff swore. "You're going to pass this one up? Are you crazy? *A hundred thousand dollars?*"

"What's money to a corpse?" Meadows eyed him coldly. "I say the odds are wrong. I say we don't do it. As of this minute, Scarff, the job is yours if you want to do it. I want no part of it, but if you go, don't come back. Not ever."

Scarff hesitated, sorely tempted. "Damn it, Harry, I didn't mean—"

"I hate to lose it, too. But take it from me, Matt Coburn won't go easy. I've seen a man like him soak up lead the way a sponge soaks up water. And when he goes he'll take somebody with him. I don't want it to be me."

"What'll we do?" Kendrick asked.

"We'll leave now, and we'll ride for Sacramento Station. We'll stay outside there in the cedars and watch what happens. If there's a chance, we'll take it."

They started, and with fresh horses and a start of five miles on the coach they made it easily. Harry Meadows was a man who knew the country, and he led them into a tiny copse well back of the station but within two minutes' riding to the station door. And the view there was good.

"Four riders," Scarff reported after a minute. "And they're no cowhands. Those men are loaded for bear meat, and riding some real horse flesh."

Harry Meadows stared at him. "You mean somebody else is going to try? But how could they know?"

He crawled up on the rock from which the station yard could be plainly seen.

The station was a long, low building. Close by were corrals, and the ruins of a stone building that had been a previous station, burned by Indians.

The horses were tied in plain sight, and they were certainly no ordinary horses. The men who rode those mounts wanted something with speed and bottom, and these were superb animals.

Only one man was in sight. Harry Meadows leveled his glasses at him, and then swore. Scarff said, "What is it, boss?"

"That's Tucker Dolan down there."

Scarff lifted his head, staring down at the dark figure that leaned against the doorpost, watching the yard. Tucker Dolan had been a deputy sheriff up in Oregon, and after that in Idaho. He had also been a hired gun for the big cattle outfits back in Texas. He was no outlaw, but his activities had often skirted the very edge of crime.

Meadows handed the glasses over to Scarff. "Somebody you know," he said.

A second man had emerged from the door, a toothpick between his lips. He was a slim man with catlike movements ... Bob Longer. Another tough man, another gun for hire, an occasional outlaw who had never been caught at it. Scarff had made a cattle drive up from Texas with him. He was a hard man, and a disagreeable one, a good worker, but a trouble-hunter.

"What the hell *is* this?" Scarff wondered out loud.

"Somebody wants a scalp," Meadows said, "and by the power they've got, they must want Coburn."

Two more men, unknown to the watchers, came out of the station, and after a heads-together conference one of them walked toward the corner of the corral, while the other stepped around the side of the house and waited there, out of sight from the road.

Meadows and his men heard the stage coming. "Are we in or out?" Kendrick asked.

"Out," Meadows said, "unless they take the gold. If they do that we hit them, quick and hard, from ambush."

"Them?"

"Right after a fight, in which they'll get hurt, they won't be expecting anything. We'll move against them."

Scarff did not like it, but he said nothing, and neither did the others. They had learned to trust Meadows' judgement.

Of the presence of Harry Meadows, and his men, Coburn knew nothing. He had his shotgun in his hands and ready when they swung into the yard. He knew Tucker Dolan at once, and he also recognized Bob Longer. And there were four horses, which meant two others somewhere about.

Half turning, he pounded three sharp blows on the top of the stage, and then as the stage drew into the yard he told Burke, "Out from the buildings, Dandy. Stop her right here. If I go down, hit them with the whip and take her out of here."

The stage swung up, the following dust cloud closing

in and settling around it. In one easy movement, Matt Coburn swung to the ground.

"Hello, Dolan," he said. "It's been a coon's age."

Tucker Dolan was surprised. He had had no idea that Matt Coburn would be riding shotgun. "I didn't know you were in this part of the country," he said.

"We're changing horses, Tucker. You interested?"

"I don't know what you're carrying, Matt, and you know I'm not riding the owl-hoot. I came to meet a passenger of yours."

Madge Healy! Why?

The stage creaked ever so slightly. A shifting of weight inside? Or somebody getting down?

"I hope it isn't trouble, Dolan. I wouldn't want that. Our passengers are to be delivered in safety."

Tucker Dolan straightened up from the door where he stood and walked just to the edge of the awning shadow. Bob Longer took a long, easy step to the right.

"Is Madge Healy aboard?" Dolan asked.

The stage door opened, and Madge stepped down. She held her purse in her left hand. Her right hand gathered her skirts. All of this Matt saw from the corner of his eye.... Did that hand among the folds of the skirt hold a gun?

"Yes, gentlemen? Is there something I can do for you?"

"You have some papers, ma'am," Tucker Dolan said. "We were sent to pick them up."

Dunning and Kearns were getting down. Charlie Kearns's face was drawn and stiff. Dunning seemed merely curious.

"Any papers I have," Madge said, "are my own. The property they represent was bought with my own money, by me. Nobody—and I mean nobody—has any rights or share in them."

"I ain't here to argue, ma'am. I was sent to get them papers. I aim to do just that."

"An' we can do it," Longer said. "We got the edge."

Two more men had stepped into view. Meadows had

not known them, but Matt Coburn did. Claim-jumpers, strike-breakers, thorough toughs. Medley and Parsons. He knew them both.

Pike Sides stepped from behind the stage. "Maybe not, Bob," he said. Without turning his head, he went on, "Coburn, if they open the ball, I want Longer an' Parsons."

Matt Coburn still held the shotgun. It was loaded with buckshot, and he knew what it could do to a man. "Madge Healy is my passenger, gentlemen," he said; "she is Wells Fargo's passenger. I don't know who paid you, but whatever you're getting it won't be enough."

"I figure you must be packin' Wells Fargo gold," Dolan said, "or they wouldn't have you on the box, Coburn. Now, we don't want any part of your gold. We ain't holdup men. We don't even want the Lady. We just want them papers." And he added, "One man has died for them, a'ready."

"Sorry," Coburn replied. "I have told you that Miss Healy is a Wells Fargo passenger. Now, gentlemen, I am through waiting. This coach has a schedule and we are going to keep to it. Dolan, this is an express gun, if you haven't noticed. At this range I can cut you right in two, and there isn't a thing in God's world could save you. Even if you got a bullet into me, or two, I'd still have your guts spread all over the ground there.

"Now, I'm not worried about Pike Sides. You all know him, and we know you. You're a tough, game lot of boys who could cut us up considerable. Nobody would win the fight, unless it would be Wells Fargo an' Miss Healy here.

"But suppose you did win? No matter what your reason, or whether you touched the gold or not, you'd be outlaws, and they'd hang you. Wells Fargo wouldn't sit still about it. And suppose Miss Healy should get shot? That they'd surely hang you for."

Tucker Dolan hesitated. Every word Matt had said was true, and he knew it. He also knew what that shotgun could do, and he had been giving it some thought. No man in his right mind bucks a deck so stacked against him.

"All right," Dolan said, "you've got us over a barrel. But that boy Madge Healy killed was the nephew of a mighty important man, and as her husband's heir, those papers belong to him."

"You'd better get some legal advice," Matt replied. "In the meanwhile, you boys just mount up and ride out of here."

Bob Longer laughed cynically. "Ride? Who rides? Who's got who? The minute you put down that shotgun I'm going to cut you into doll rags."

"Pike!" Matt spoke sharply and tossed the shotgun, which Pike caught deftly.

"All right, Bob," Matt's tone was even. "I'm not holding the shotgun now."

Bob Longer looked across the intervening thirty feet at Matt Coburn. This was the old bull of the woods. This was the man they said was the toughest, the fastest, the gamest of them all. Longer went for his gun.

The watchers saw him move, the listeners heard only one sound. Bob Longer felt the quick, sharp tug at his shirt pocket. His gun was moving. In his mind a single thought: *he was going to kill . . . he was going to kill . . . to kill . . . kill . . .*

And then he was dead.

There was the acrid smell of gunpowder; wind rustled the leaves of a cottonwood beside the stage station. One of the horses tugged nervously at the bit, rattling his harness.

"He wasn't going to stand, Dolan," Matt said. "He was making a fight of it."

"Yeah," Tucker Dolan said bitterly, "but if you'd kept that shotgun he'd still be alive."

For an instant Matt Coburn stood perfectly still. "He was asking for it," he said then.

"That he was," Dolan agreed, "an' he would have killed somebody or been killed by somebody, no matter what. Only you needn't have done it."

Matt Coburn faced around on him. "Are you riding, Dolan? Are you other boys riding out of here?"

"Yes, we're ridin'," Dolan said.

He walked up to his horse, followed by the others. As they mounted up, Coburn indicated Longer. "What about him?"

"You bury him. He's your meat."

When they were gone Madge Healy walked across the yard to the station and sat down abruptly at the first table inside the door. Her knees were shaking, and she felt faint and sick.

Matt Coburn held out his hand toward Pike and the gunman tossed him the shotgun. "You're quick," he said, "mighty quick."

Coburn did not reply. Horses were being brought up and Dandy Burke was busy. Dunning was sitting at the end of the overhang, elbows on his knees, head hanging.

"You'll get over it, boy," Charlie Kearns was saying. "Over in Pioche I saw three get it in no more time."

Coburn held the shotgun in the hollow of his arm and punched two empty shells from the six-shooter.

Pike saw them. "Two? *Two?*"

"Look at him," Coburn said.

Pike Sides walked to the dead man and rolled him over. There were two holes over the heart that could have been covered by a silver dollar, or even a poker chip. He swore softly. The two shots had been fired so close together they had made but one sound.

Matt Coburn stepped inside and sat down beside Madge, placing the shotgun on the table before him. From where he sat he could see the whole yard, and the approaches to it.

"Hadn't you better tell me about it, Madge?"

There was a cup of coffee in front of her. The waiter brought another for him, then went quietly away.

"I never had anybody, Matt. I never had anybody at all. When I was a youngster my aunt just used me to make money enough so she and Ed could stay drunk all the time. Nobody ever kissed me good-night, Matt. Nobody ever tucked me in. They just worked me.

"Well, I held out money my aunt didn't know about, enough from the coins they threw at me, so that I bought the horse to get away on. I had forty dollars left, I hired Mrs. Finnegan on spec, and Joe the same way.

"I made money, lots of it. I never spent much, and finally I bought a hotel and a ranch and some stock in eastern steel mills, and then I bought some mining stock. I got control of the Blue Duck."

Matt looked at her sharply. "The Blue Duck? You?"

"Yes. Willard & Kingsbury wanted it. Their lease ran out and they had been stealing from me, and they had just struck a big pocket of high-grade ore. They supposed that I didn't know." She looked at Matt. "I never had reason to trust anyone, Matt, so I'd had them spied on. One of the miners who worked for them was also paid by me. They discovered it somehow, and they murdered him, and when I would not renew their lease and put guards on the mine, they tried it another way.

"Willard had a nephew back east. He was no good, and never had been, but they sent for him to come out. He met me and he was nice. I had no idea who he was. He talked sweet to me, and I married him. All he ever wanted were the deeds, the permits, the property I had, the options I had. He got those and he ran away."

"He tried to, you mean."

"He did ... but I had a friend who saw him, who knew what he was taking, and who stopped him. He was an old man, and my husband drew a derringer on him and tried to kill him, but he was a very tough old man, and he killed my husband and brought the valise back to me."

"The Negro?"

She looked at him, hesitated, then said, "Yes. I said nothing because there are people who might have hung him for it, right or wrong. He protected me; I protected him."

"Some folks think *you* killed your husband."

"That's their problem."

"And yours?"

"Getting to Carson City and filing some of these papers. I have a lawyer there, a good one."

He studied her for a moment. "How old are you, Madge?"

"Nineteen ... going on forty. Nobody looks out for a girl alone, Matt. She looks out for herself, and you know what kind of a world it is."

He finished his coffee. "You'll be all right to Carson, Madge. We'll see you through." He paused a moment. "Is Pike Sides working for you?"

"He was one of the guards at the mine. After my husband was killed and I found out who he was and what they were trying to do, I had Pike come to meet me here. I thought I needed a bodyguard."

"You were right."

He got up. "It's time to go, Madge. We're moving out."

The body was gone, the team was hitched up, Kearns and Dunning were seated in the stage. Dandy Burke was standing by it, and Pike Sides was loafing under the awning's shade.

Matt helped Madge Healy into the stage. Sides followed but Matt hesitated, letting his eyes go up the mountain slope. Earlier there had been a gleam from up there, as if sunlight had reflected off field glasses.

There was nothing now. Of course, it might have been a bit of mica, or even quartz.

Matt swung to the seat and Burke turned the team, pulling into the trail.

Matt looked back. For the first time he thought about Bob Longer. He had not wanted to kill him, and he need not have accepted that challenge ... so why did he do it?

Tucker Dolan was right. He could have kept the shotgun and there would have been no shooting.

CHAPTER 10

The story of the shooting reached Confusion before the
stage got to Carson City. Matt Coburn had killed Bob
Longer—an attempted kidnaping, some said; others said
it was a try at robbing a passenger. The fact loomed
large that Coburn had killed another man.

Laurie Shannon had the story from Joss Ringgold over
coffee in the ranch kitchen.

"Joss, is Harry Meadows still hiding out over in the
mountains?"

"No, ma'am. He pulled his stakes. About the time the
stage left."

"Will he try to stop the stage?"

Joss hesitated. "No. I don't believe so. He will give it
some thought, then he'll pull back and tell himself no—
it's too dangerous."

"Because of Matt?"

"Matt Coburn's quick on the shoot, ma'am. Maybe too
quick."

She sat silent, staring at her coffee cup. "What's he
coming to, Joss? You know about men like that."

He shrugged. "Each one's special in himself, but once a
man starts to use a gun he has to watch himself. He gets
jumpy. He has enemies, he has reputation-huntin' kids to

86

think of, and he knows he's fair game for any man with a gun.

"Matt's a good man, but he's a hard man in a hard country. There's many a time when if you wait for the other man to draw you can get killed. When things are like that, sometimes a man figures to get them before they get him.

"Jim Gillette, Jeff Milton, Bill Tilghman ... men like that never drew a gun unless they had to. Hickok ... I knew him well. If you came to town huntin' him or huntin' trouble, you'd better not make any wrong moves or he'd shoot. Dave Mathers didn't wait for you. If you came to town talkin' loud about what you intended to do, Dave would find you and shoot you before you even got started.

"Confusion, now—Matt don't want the job, and he shouldn't have it. To run Confusion you'd have to use a gun. There's no other way. Some of that crowd know Matt and would pull out if he became marshal, some would sit quiet, and there's a good many would try to kill him. Big Thompson would—he'd have to. He's made his brags and he's made his stand, and he's run marshals out of town elsewhere, so he'd have to tackle Matt."

"What about Nathan Bly?"

"He's cold ... like ice. The most dangerous man around here, leaving out Matt Coburn and Calvin Bell. And he's made the switch. He's no longer just a good man with a gun. He's a killer."

They were silent for a few moments, and then Laurie said, "Joss, is there any red clay on the ranch? Have I missed something?"

The older man's eyes hooded. He got out his pipe and began to fill it slowly. "I guess you ain't missed a thing, ma'am," he replied quietly. "No, there's no red clay on this ranch."

"But there is, over west. I seem to remember a water hole over in the Schell Creek Mountains where there was red clay."

Joss Ringgold's eyes twinkled, but the expression faded. "You're canny, ma'am, right canny. You noticed the hocks of those horses, too, didn't you?"

"Freeman and that man who was supposedly carrying the mail to Confusion. Joss, is Free getting into trouble?"

"He's a hard-headed youngster. Thinks he knows it all. And he figures he's pretty handy with that gun."

"Is he?"

"Oh, he gets it out pretty fast. He might kill somebody. He's just a-achin' and a-sweatin' to be a big man. If he killed somebody he'd likely turn mean and even more big-headed than he is now. But he won't—not 'less the man's drunk. He wouldn't last out the year."

"That man who said he was carrying mail ... did you know him, Joss?"

"I've seen him around. Nobody I know of would trust him with the mail. Took me a while to recall him—name of Scarff. Last I heard, he had joined up with Harry Meadows."

"That's what I was afraid of. Will he listen to you, Joss? Freeman, I mean?"

"I doubt it."

Ringgold got to his feet. "Ma'am, it ain't my place to get personal, but I'm old enough to be your pa. If you're gettin' a case on Matt Coburn ... don't. He's turnin' bad."

After Joss had gone back to work, Laurie Shannon sat for a long time, thinking.

Was she getting a case on Matt Coburn? Laurie prided herself on being a cool-headed girl who stood for no nonsense from herself, and now she faced her feelings squarely.

Was she? That was just it—she did not know. At first it had been his sheer masculinity that impressed her, that and his quietness, the easy way he moved, the gentleness with which he treated his horse. And then it had been his loneliness.

During the time when he was out in the hills alone she had often found herself lying awake at night wondering what he was doing, where he was, and how it must feel to be always alone. She had been much alone herself, and thought she knew but there was a difference.

After a few minutes she dismissed the idea from her mind. She *could* get a case on him, as Joss put it, but she was not likely to see enough of him. And she was not going to permit it—not for one minute.

Yet an hour later she was thinking of him out there on the box of that stage, fair game for any sharpshooter with a good rifle.

Matt Coburn buttoned the two top buttons of his coat. It had been hot earlier; now the day was cooling off. In just a little while they would be changing teams again. For the last hour they had been traveling across the open country, but he had not relaxed the least bit. Almost automatically his hand went to his cartridge belt and loosened a pair of shotgun shells to have them ready if needed.

They rode now with the sun before them, with the shadows rounding up in the secret draws of the mountains, and here and there a lonely stray behind some isolated butte. The team moved slowly now, Burke holding them in for the time later when he might wish to get speed from them. The sound of their hoofs, the jingle of harness, and the rocking, creaking, rolling of the coach, these were the sounds.

Far off across the basin, a last dust devil died in the valley, and a cool wind came down from the peaks, rich with the smell of cedar and pine.

Dandy Burke guided the six horses as if they were one, easing the coach over the worst of the bumps, rolling into the dips, walking up the slopes beyond.

He pointed toward the mountains with his whipstock. "I'm going into those hills someday, and I'm going to stay. I'm going to trace one of those canyons back to the high country beyond, and make myself a home there."

"I've been thinking of it, too."

"You eat dust for twenty years, you eat it behind trail

drives and stagecoach teams, and finally you've had enough. I want to go where there's tall pines and cool water. I've had enough of alkali and dodging lead."

"I've found a place I'm thinking about, back there near the foot of Jeff Davis," Matt said. "There's always water."

"You ought to find youself a woman. A man should marry, Matt, and *you* should."

"Why me?"

Burke lifted the reins and let the horses trot down an easy slope. "You're getting mean, Matt. You've lived with a gun too long."

"What was I supposed to do? Let Bob Longer jump me in a saloon some day? Or take a shot at me in the dark? I could read it in him. He had to kill me ... and he'd have tried. Then or later."

They were silent then, and after a while, Coburn took out his pipe. "You're right, Dandy," he said. "I'm too touchy. I've seen it building up in me, but I sleep with a gun, I eat with a gun in my lap, I never take a step without one. I never go to sleep at night that I don't expect to wake up shooting. And I almost never sleep in the same place twice ... not if I can help it."

"I know," Burke said. And he did know. He had seen it in Matt, and in others, too. It was easier to give the advice than to carry it out. Once you've lived that life, once you've had it to think about, you never quite lose the feeling.

It was like hunting Apaches, or traveling in Apache country, and Matt Coburn had lived that life too. You learned never to sleep soundly, no matter how tired you were. You learned to cook your food, put out your fire, and move on a few miles before settling down for the night. You learned to look for shadows where shadows should not be, to watch for the out-of-the-way thing, to expect the unexpected.

The day passed, and a long night, and then another day. The trails were dusty, the passengers tired, and short-tempered.

While the horses rested at the top of a steep grade, the passengers got down to stretch their legs. The country was wide open in all directions. Dandy Burke checked his harness and the horses, then bit off a chew of tobacco.

Matt Coburn found himself standing beside Madge Healy. "Where are we going to stop, Matt?" she asked. "I mean, so we can rest a little?"

"In Eureka," he said.

"It's a lively place. I played the opera house there. And I played it a few years before that when the stage was four planks laid over some barrels."

"Why did you quit?"

"I just got tired of it, Matt. I wanted a home so bad I cried myself to sleep many a night. I used to hide money the miners threw to me, and whenever my aunt found it, she'd whip me. But I still did it.

"Once, when I was only fifteen, I grubstaked a prospector I met in Austin. Everybody was turning him down ... I heard them and felt sorry for him. I grubstaked him with just thirty dollars I'd held out, and later I sent him forty more."

"Did you ever see him again?"

She smiled. "That prospector's name was Charley Ramona," she said quietly. "He struck it pretty good, sold out, bought stock in the Denver & Rio Grande, and made a mint of money."

"How did you make out?"

She looked up at Matt. "I own half of it," she said, smiling at him. "Willard & Kingsbury don't know that, Matt. When they picked a fight with me they thought I was just a little girl with a fluttery head. I didn't ask for the fight, but I'll own *them* before I'm through, Matt, and that's the first boast I ever made, I think."

"Serve them right. But you be careful. Willard is mean enough, but I know Kingsbury—he's worse."

They stood close together, watching the shadows creeping over the land.

"Matt, what about Pike Sides?" Madge asked suddenly. "Do you know him?"

"Enough."

"Can he be trusted? I mean, will he sell out?"

"No. Once you've hired him, he's your man, but don't make a mistake, Madge. Pike is a whip that can be cracked to make people move, but don't ever let him get a-hold of the handle."

"Thanks, Matt. And thanks again for back there. It was you who stopped them. They'd have killed me, Matt. I know they would have. Bob Longer was the one who would have done it—as if it was an accident."

He looked surprised.

"Yes, I knew Longer was hired to do just that. Dolan didn't know anything about that. It was purely Longer."

Now the stage started again, picked up its dust cloud, and rolled west. When they came to Eureka they found it was lively and wide open. There were a hundred and twenty-five saloons, fifteen tent shows, and twenty-five gambling houses, all of them going strong.

Matt was tired. Every muscle sagged with weariness, and his eyes were red-rimmed from staring at the bright, sunlit land. When he swung down from the stage at the Colonnade Hotel, Pike was already helping Madge Healy to the ground.

"Pike?"

The gunman turned his eyes upon him. "They'll be in town," Matt said. "They still want her, and they want those papers."

"Thanks," Pike said shortly. "You handle your business, an' I'll handle mine."

"That's all right, Pike," Madge said. "I value Mr. Coburn's suggestions. What is it, Matt?"

He stepped closer, so only she and Pike could hear. "Get a room, then move into a different one. They'll come hunting, you can bet on it."

"All right, Matt." She looked up at him, her face partly in the shadow. One hand touched his sleeve. "Thanks."

Dandy Burke helped Matt lower the gold box to the ground. Together they carried it inside and took a room on the ground floor, back of the office.

"Go ahead and eat," Burke said. "I'll hold the fort. Bring me a sandwich and some coffee when you come back. You tap twice very light, then once hard. I'll open up then if it's your voice."

Matt handed Burke the shotgun and stepped outside, closing the door. He stood still and glanced in each direction along the corridor. At one end was the door to the lobby of the hotel; at the other end of the passage was a door that opened onto an alley. He walked back to it, listened, and then opened the door and, after a glance, stepped out.

After studying the street with care, he walked down to a small restaurant, where he took a table in the back. Seated with his back to the wall, and facing the door, he ate a good meal.

When he left he walked through the kitchen and used the back door to get out. He stopped by several of the saloons, merely glancing in over the doors, and then going on. With the quick skill of a man who had been marshal of more than one town, he was able to assay at a glance the people inside the saloons.

As he went along the street, he almost automatically scanned the brands on the horses, and studied the rigs and their contents. Any town marshal worth his salt could in a few minutes detect the presence of strangers, of long riders, or drifters, even in a town that was strange to him.

Matt knew Eureka from past experience, and the men who were here, like those who were now in Confusion, had been known to him in other camps, either by name or reputation. And each one bore the stamp of his kind, whether he realized it or not.

Matt was looking for potential trouble, and he found it. In the fourth saloon he saw Harry Meadows leaning against the bar. He walked in and stopped alongside Meadows.

"I'll buy a drink, Harry," Matt said.

"Go ahead. It's your money." And Meadows straightened a little as he spoke, to stand taller beside the taller man. He turned, leaning one elbow on the bar. "You had you some grief."

"Was that you up on the rock?" Matt asked evenly.

"Uh-huh." Meadows picked up his drink. "I had me a Winchester, too."

"I figured you did. I'd never worry about you, Harry. Not that way. You're just not the type."

Harry Meadows, who was honest with himself, was not sure just what this meant, but he was pleased. "Who was it down there?" he asked. "Bob Longer?"

"Yeah."

"He's been leadin' up to it." Meadows turned his glass, tracing a ring on the bar. "You goin' all the way to Carson with it?"

"Uh-huh. Pike Sides, too. He's riding shotgun for Madge Healy."

Meadows was puzzled. "Madge? The kid actress? That dancer?"

"Yeah, only she isn't a kid any longer, and she has enemies. Her enemies are Willard & Kingsbury."

"She's in trouble, then." Meadows was silent for a few minutes, and then he said, "Matt, I always liked that kid. She gave a lot of entertainment where there wasn't anybody else, and she'd dance until she dropped if the boys asked for it. And you've always been a square-shooter."

"What are you getting at?"

"Willard & Kingsbury. They've been hiring. I don't know what the deal is, but a couple of my boys have been approached. They want men who aren't afraid of a fight, a dirty fight. Ike Fletcher has been hiring for them."

Ike Fletcher was a claim-jumper, a dangerous man in any kind of a fight. If he was hiring men, the chances were it was some kind of a mine fight.

"Where are they going?"

"I don't know, but my guess would be Confusion. One of my boys doesn't want to go to Arizona. He's wanted there, and in Colorado too. When he told them that they said he wouldn't have to worry. He wouldn't be traveling far."

Matt finished his drink. He had been in the saloon about as long as he ever allowed himself to be in one. "Harry, I've got to drift." He put his glass down. "I hope I don't see you again for a while."

Meadows grinned. "Now, that ain't a threat, is it, Matt?"

"You know better. Fact is, the way I think about you, I wouldn't like to look over a gun at you."

"You won't get the chance, Matt, not even for that hundred thousand you're carrying. If anybody bothers you, remember this: it won't be me."

Matt turned, gave a quick glance around the room and went out, looking neither to right nor left. Only a fool goes looking for trouble, and his life had brought him more than enough, and knowing how to recognize possible trouble meant knowing how to avoid it. Even to meet the glance of some men was an invitation to trouble, for to them it was a challenge to which they must respond.

This watchfulness in Matt was no new thing, but it was something that had been growing in him with the realization that not only had he enemies, but that being a known gunfighter made him fair game for anyone. He knew that men who killed gunfighters or gunmen, no matter what the conditions, were rarely punished for it.

Back at the hotel, Matt entered by the front door, and went along to get several sandwiches, a pot of coffee, and cups. With these he went back to the room and rapped at the door with the arranged signal.

Dandy Burke was seated in a chair tilted against the wall facing the door. The shotgun was across his knees.

"Figured you'd forgotten me,' he grumbled. "It seemed a long time."

"I saw Harry Meadows. He won't bother us."

Burke looked up sharply. "I didn't hear any shootin'."

"We talked, that was all. Meadows wants to win. That's why he's still around. The man never took an unnecessary chance in his life. Too many crooks think things are going to be just the way they would like them to be. He'll take the stage some day when there's less money on it, and no guard—or somebody else than me or Eugene Blair. Nobody wants to deal with Blair."

"I drove with him a couple of times."

Burke ate, and then stretched out on the cot. Almost at once he was asleep. Matt tilted back in his chair, and kept the room dark. He finished the coffee, ate the sandwich Burke had left, and after that he took off his boots and coat. He was hanging up his coat when he heard somebody try the knob.

"Go ahead," he said quietly, "if you feel lucky."

The floor creaked, and there was silence. Prospecting, he thought—just somebody prospecting a little.

CHAPTER 11

At Austin they were joined by Hank Weber, and the coach rolled on, with Weber driving and Burke sleeping inside. Thunder rolled, rains lashed the coach, flash floods ripped the trail asunder, but somehow the drivers found a way around and the coach kept moving. Through it all, Matt Coburn rode the top, sleeping when stops were made if it was possible, but always alert.

They reached Carson City and the gold was delivered. Madge Healy got down from the stage, Pike Sides standing near.

"Matt," she said, "can I ride back with you?"

He looked at her, his eyes red-rimmed and weary. "You know you can. And if you have trouble here you send for me."

"I'll handle any trouble," Pike cut in. "She won't need anybody else."

"The offer stands," Matt responded.

"I'll remember," Madge said. Her eyes were soft as she looked at him. "Thanks, Matt. I don't have many friends."

"You will have. You were loyal to that old man, the one who got your papers back. Loyalty brings friends, Madge."

He stood there on the street, a lonely man, watching

her go. Tucker Dolan joined him. "I'm out of a job," he said wryly. "They didn't like the way it was handled."

"They should try it themselves," Matt said. "Have you heard anything about them hiring fighters?"

Dolan gave him a quick glance. "It's trouble, Matt, real trouble. They didn't want me. I guess I wasn't bloody enough, but they've hired Kendrick and some others. I'd say they've got fifteen tough men."

"Do you know why?"

"No . . . they don't tell us anything. All I know is that Madge Healy is the center of it. Did you know she was in the mining game?"

"Up to her pretty ears," Matt replied.

"Then she'd better get out of it. They'll eat her alive."

"Don't bet on it." Matt looked hard at Dolan. "Are you going back to Confusion? If you do, stick around a few days. I may have a deal for you. I may need a tough man who can stand still for trouble, and who doesn't go off half-cocked."

Matt slept that afternoon and through most of the night. When he woke before daybreak the town was quiet. A light tapping came at the door.

Madge Healy stood there when he opened it. She stepped in quickly. "Put on your pants, Matt. You look like the devil in those long johns."

"I wasn't expecting a lady."

"Thanks for the compliment. I try to be a lady, but sometimes it isn't easy. Matt, I want to go back to Confusion. I want to go now, and I want to go fast."

"We weren't figuring on making a run for it," Matt said. "We had that, remember?"

"It has to be that way, Matt. Things are getting rough, and they're going to get worse."

Briefly, he told her what he had heard from Harry Meadows, and from Tucker Dolan. She listened in silence. After a moment she walked across to the window as he hurriedly splashed water on his face, combed his hair and put on a shirt.

"I didn't know it had gone that far, Matt. but you're

one of the few friends I've got. Matt, I own the Treasure Vault, and I own other claims. They're big and they're rich. Willard & Kingsbury have moved in on me. They bought the Balzac from Big Thompson—"

"I thought Frenchy Bezant owned it."

"When did that ever stop Thompson? He picked a fight with Frenchy and killed him."

"So?"

"They're claiming that my Treasure Vault is on their Balzac vein."

"Is Pike still with you?"

"Yes."

He buckled on his guns. "All right, Madge. Let's get Burke and Weber."

She looked up at him. "They're over there already with the team, Matt, or should be. I was sure you'd help, so I sent Pike to round them up."

The team was hitched when Matt came walking up, shotgun in hand. He helped Madge into the coach and Pike Sides walked out of the barn and got in beside her, with Weber. Matt swung up and Burke cracked his whip. The stage started with a lunge. It rolled up the draw, and turned along the hillside toward the temporary Wells Fargo office.

In Austin they picked up another passenger. James Hoyt was a mining engineer working out of Denver, representing various New York investment houses from time to time. It had been several years since he had seen Madge Healy perform, and he did not recognize the young woman who sat opposite him. She, however, knew him at once, and was familiar with mining-camp gossip and knew his business.

"Do you often travel in the west" she asked demurely.

"Oh, yes. My company sends me out to investigate properties they contemplate buying, or in which they might invest."

"I don't know much about Confusion," she said. "Is it really a serious mining town? I mean, are the mines there any good?"

"Some of them, I expect. The samples of ore I've seen showed excellent values."

Gently, she led him on to talk of his work, bringing him back again and again to Confusion. Finally he said, "I will not be there very long. Perhaps we might go for a drive? I could show you the country, and if you are interested in mining I could explain the geology to you."

"I'd love that!"

Pike Sides had been looking out the window, but now he turned his head to look at her, puzzled by her act of innocence.

"Do you have only one mine to consider?" she asked. "I heard there was a very rich one there, the Discovery, I think they called it." She paused. "Are you actually going to buy a mine?"

"As a matter of fact," Hoyt said, "I might buy or invest. I have the authority here." He tapped his coat pocket.

He was aware he was talking too much, but Pike was obviously just a drifting gunman, and this girl—she was scarcely more than a child—was so interested. Not in mines, he was sure, so it must be in himself. He expanded a little, talking easily of ores, drifts, hanging walls, and timbering, and Madge listened, her eyes wide and beautiful.

"I love to hear a man talk about what he is interested in," she said. "One learns so much! And I love the names of the mines! I wonder where they get all those names?"

The ride from Austin to Confusion was a long and dusty one, and Pike Sides soon fell asleep. In the intimacy of the coach, sitting opposite a beautiful girl, James Hoyt continued to talk. Among other things he advised her to keep off the streets in Confusion—there might be some shooting, he believed. It seemed there was some argument over claims and over who held them. But he was going to the town to check on several.

Again Madge brought up the subject of names, and Hoyt mentioned the Treasure Vault. "As a matter of fact," he said, "if it measures up to the assays, we expect to buy it from the new owners."

"So you won't be in town long?"

"I'm leaving the twelfth," Hoyt said. "Can we take our drive before then?"

"We will have to see. I will be living on a ranch. I have a friend there"—she picked the name up quickly—"a young woman named Laurie Shannon. Do you know of her?"

"I know the name." Hoyt was reassured. He did know the name, and knew that the Shannon girl lived on a ranch and had no concern with mines or mining.

When the stage drew to a halt before the Wells Fargo office in Confusion, Newt Clyde stepped up to meet it. Matt Coburn swung down first, then Pike Sides. Hoyt stepped down and helped Madge to the ground. "By the way," he said, "I don't even know your name."

She smiled up at him. "It's Healy," she said sweetly, "Madge Healy."

His face stiffened. He knew of Madge Healy, but he had thought of her as older, harder, and not nearly so attractive. He vaguely remembered hearing of Madge Healy in connection with several mining towns. He had thought—

"I see," he said awkwardly.

She smiled brightly. "I hope you do, Mr. Hoyt—it will save you and your firm a lot of money and a lot of trouble. Willard & Kingsbury do not own the Treasure Vault, and they will never own it."

She turned away abruptly and, accompanied by a grinning Pike Sides, walked down the street, with Hoyt staring after them.

"That—that is Madge Healy? She isn't dry behind the ears yet!"

Matt smiled. "It seems to me you just found out different. And take my advice—believe what she told you."

"I came a long way to make that deal," Hoyt replied with some uncertainty, "and my people aren't going to like it if I don't close it."

"They'll like it less if you lose their shirt," Clyde observed dryly.

Matt Coburn looked down the dusty street. Along the edges of the buildings some desert growth remained, and somebody had taken the time to dig the rocks from the street. In front of several of the buildings a crude boardwalk had been built, but the street itself needed considerably more work.

He knew the sounds of such towns. Each had its own tone, its own particular hum. Though the shadings might be different, the sounds were the same—the pound of a compressor or a stamp mill, the sound of hammers, the squeak and rattle of a pump or a windlass. The tin-panny sounds of the music boxes or pianos, the strident, unmusical voices singing, the rattle of glasses, loud voices raised in argument, the crash of broken glass, the noise of wheels rolling and bumping over rocks, the creak of saddle leather, the hoof-falls, the sounds of hard heels on the boardwalks ... The sounds were the same, and he could wake at almost any hour and know the time just by the sounds.

He knew, too, the sound of trouble coming, he could feel it in the air, just as a wild animal feels the coming of a storm. And he could feel it now. This town was coming apart at the seams.

He had seen towns come, and he had seen them go. Some had died a-borning from too much law or too much religion, some had committed suicide from lack of any law at all; some the changing of trails had killed, and some had died from water-filled shafts, from the playing out of ore ... some from lack of faith.

In this town the lawlessness had been casual, caused by a few men who were violent—some deliberately so, some simply because of too much liquor, too much need to let off steam. So far, some men had been callous, others had been heedless, some few had been deliberately murderous. Now it was beginning to change. There was nothing to put a damper on the town, and now it was edging toward anarchy.

A few strong men might weld a city government, pass laws, stand firmly behind them, and bring law without gunplay if they moved quickly before things got out of hand.

But not here—not in Confusion. Matt Coburn knew the kind of men along that street, and he knew there was only one way to run this town now. You had to run it with a gun—a gun you could use, and they knew you would use.

Any slight move now, he was thinking, might jar the whole town into an explosive madness. There were a few men who could trigger the movement, and with some of them it might be unintentional. Most of those here wanted to operate lawlessly, but even their lawlessness must function within the pattern.

"You like this town?" he asked Clyde.

The Wells Fargo man shrugged. "They come and they go. I've seen a lot of towns, and I'll see a lot more. This is the Discovery town. It belongs to Felton, Cohan, and Zeller."

"Then tell them to move quick or they've lost it," Matt said. "That bunch down there are ready to blow the lid off. Most of them will be sorry afterwards, but they'll do it."

Felton and Cohan came along to join them, and Coburn explained about the fighters being recruited. "They've planned to jump the Treasure Vault."

Newton Clyde lit his cigar. "I am the Wells Fargo man. If you have gold to ship, I will ship it. Wells Fargo does not build towns nor enforce the law . . . except along the stage routes."

"What would you suggest, Matt?" Cohan asked.

"A citizen's committee. Twelve to twenty tough, honest men who will stand their ground and will shoot if need be. Then an ultimatum. If legal action will not work, use lever action, administer your law with Winchesters. Start a local uplift society, and use a rope to do the lifting. I know this crowd, and they understand nothing else."

"I don't believe that," Felton protested.

"It's your town," Matt Coburn said. "You can believe what you like. Why don't you just walk down the street and ask Big Thompson why he doesn't behave? Ask him to hang up his guns and get a job."

Felton flushed, and started to speak, but Coburn ignored him. "How many killings have you had so far?" he asked.

"Eighteen," Cohan replied, "in thirty-some days. Not all of them right in town, though."

"And how many robberies?"

"Who can count them? Most of them aren't even reported."

"We want no more violence," Felton said stubbornly. "There just has to be another way."

"Men like Thompson and Gorman—yes, and Willard & Kingsbury, for that matter—just love people who don't believe in violence. It gives them a free hand because they not only believe in it, they use it. Ask Madge Healy."

Several of the townsmen had gathered around them, listening. "What would you do, Cohan," Matt Coburn asked, "if somebody tried to jump the Discovery?"

"I'd fight. What else could I do?"

"Undt me," Zeller rumbled. "I fight also."

"There you are, Felton. There's two men for your committee." Coburn glanced around at Gage. "How about you?"

"No," Gage replied stiffly. "Leave me out of it. I have seen these towns come and go. When I can no longer do business, I will leave. Why risk my neck for what will be nothing but a rubbish pile in a few years?"

"Buckwalter?"

"There will be another town. I have only one neck."

"I'm a fool," Clyde said, "but I'll serve on your committee. "I'll do it just to run that bunch out."

"No," Felton insisted. "It is not necessary. This will all blow over. It'll settle down."

Coburn shrugged. "Well, it isn't my affair. I am riding out of town. I delivered your gold, Felton. I will take my money and go."

Clyde was staring at him, and so were Gage and Buckwalter. Cohan was about to speak, but he kept quiet.

Felton took five gold coins from his pocket and put them in Coburn's hand. "Thanks, Coburn. You did a good job."

Matt walked to the livery stable and led out his horse. Dandy Burke joined him. "You aren't going to take the job?"

"Nobody has offered me the job, and I don't want it." He picked up his saddle and threw it on the gelding's back. "That's a mean bunch down there, Dandy, maybe the meanest I ever saw. And there isn't much time."

Across the street the huddle of men watched him. Clyde took the stub of his cigar from his lips and studied it distastefully. "There he goes, gentlemen. The only man who can bring peace to your town. The only man who can hold it together."

"Nonsense!" Felton spoke sharply. "I started this town, and—"

"And you'll see the finish of it."

Buckwalter spoke quietly. "I say hire him, Felton. Newt's right. If you don't hire him I am going to close down. I will load up and move out. I'd rather take a small loss then see all I own go up in flames."

Felton could not believe him. He looked from him to Gage. "Are you serious? You really mean you'd pull out? Why, you've only just got here!"

"Felton, you haven't been in his country long," Buckwalter said. "Did you ever hear of Fessenden?"

"No."

"Fessenden started off about like this. The mines not as rich, not quite as many people there. They killed two marshals, and nobody else would take the job. For a few days the town got wilder and wilder, and then one night Peggoty Gorman wanted a drink and the bartender was down at the other end of the bar, so Peg walked around the end of the bar and picked up a bottle. Then he tossed another bottle to a pal of his.

"The bartender saw what was happening and came running down the bar and grabbed at Peg, and Peg hit him across the face with the bottle. When the bartender fell, Peggoty kicked him a few times, and then he began tossing bottles to his friends.

"I was there," Buckwalter added, "and I just eased toward the door, got out, and went up the street. Most of my stuff had not arrived yet, so I tossed what I had in the back of a buckboard. By the time I'd done that the crowd had stripped the first saloon and started on the second. Some of them were ripping a store apart to take what they could; others had started on the dance hall.

"I didn't try to get to the main trail—I knew I'd be foolish to try. I just started up the slope behind the town on the trail to a claim. I warned the boys there, and drove on to pick up the trail on the ridge beyond. When I looked back the town was in flames."

"Why didn't they send for Coburn, if he's all that mighty?"

"Oh, they sent for him, all right," Buckwalkter said. "When he got there the ashes were still smoking. There were a couple of claims starting to work again, but the nearest mill was fifty miles away, and the nearest post office too. Nobody ever came back."

Felton was silent. Everything within his nature rebelled at the thought of violence, of hiring a gunfighter to clean up the town, his town. There had to be another way. Moreover—and he was honest enough to admit it—he did not want Matt Coburn in town. Was it because of Laurie Shannon?

"How about it, Dick?" Cohan suggested. "Shall we try to hire him?"

"No," Felton said. "I will be the marshal. I will do it myself, and alone."

They stared at him, disbelief in their eyes, and as they stared they heard the sound of Matt Coburn's horse riding over the ridge, away from town.

CHAPTER 12

Matt Coburn rode into the yard at the Rafter LS, and the first person he saw was Joss Ringgold. The old man nodded. "Howdy, Matt." He straightened up from the bridle he was mending, glancing toward the house. "Heard you had trouble down the trail."

"Some." Matt swung down and tied his horse. "You boys been doin' any traveling?"

"None to speak of. Free took him a ride over to Strawb'ry after strays. Didn't find any."

"Seems unlikely cattle would stray off this range," Coburn commented. "You got good grass, good water."

"Scarff rode in." Ringgold seemed to be just making talk, but he did not know what was in the wind, and he liked Matt Coburn. Besides, he did not want any man shot in the back. "Told us he seen some of our stuff over thataway."

Scarff . . . and the last Matt Coburn had heard of Scarff he was riding with Harry Meadows. He was quite sure in his own mind that the rider he had seen streaking it for Meadows' hide-out had been Free Dorset, and then he had seen Dorset at Strawberry. There was a pattern there somewhere, if he could only make it out. In any event, it looked as if something was going on

108

between Dorset and Harry Meadows ... and Dorset wasn't seasoned enough for Meadows. So ... ?

Laurie Shannon appeared in the doorway. "Matt! I thought I heard your voice. What are you doing over here?"

He grinned at her. "Ridin' the grub line, Laurie. Figured you might have a cup of coffee for a driftin' man."

"Surest thing you know. Joss, do you want a cup?"

"Maybe later, ma'am."

"Where's Free?" Laurie asked.

"Over to Horse Heaven, scoutin' grass. Ain't likely he'll be back before sundown."

Matt sank into his chair, suddenly relieved. He did not want to see Freeman Dorset. He did not want to cope with whatever that young man represented. He simply wanted to rest.

It was shadowed and cool in the ranch kitchen, and he liked the smell of the coffee, liked to see Laurie moving about. Slowly the tension went out of him. He sipped the coffee and felt his muscles relax. Only here did he feel at ease, only here could he completely let go. Whatever else Laurie Shannon had done, she had built a place of security and comfort.

"How did you do it?" he asked suddenly. "Build this place, I mean?"

She held the coffeepot in her hand, gazing out of the window. Then she shrugged a little. "It was what I wanted—it is as simple as that. We had a home in Ireland, a lovely place. I never knew until later that we didn't own it ... it was only a tenant's cottage. We came over to the States when I was seven, and we settled in Pennsylvania, where pa worked in a mill. He was a wild Irishman, all right, but underneath he was quite canny. He saved a bit of money, brought us west, and then he worked on the railroad. After a while we went on to Oregon, where we had a farm. Ma died and I kept house for pa and my brothers, and then pa was killed in a logging accident.

"The farm had come to be worth something, and the

cattle too. We sold the farm and split the money amongst us, and I kept forty head for breeding stock. I moved more than once, and then I found this place ... and here I'll stay."

She sat down opposite him. "Our first cattle were Durhams, then we bought a small herd of longhorns, and by the time I settled here I had some good mixed stock, as you've seen."

She looked up at him suddenly. "What are you going to do, Matt? Are you going to straighten out their town for them?"

"No."

"Is it true that Madge Healy rode to Carson with you?"

"Yes. There's a big outfit—mine speculators—who are trying to get some property away from her. Believe me, they picked the wrong girl."

"What's she like, Matt? Is she beautiful?"

"There's no doubt about that, I guess. Maybe you'd say she was striking. She's a lady, Laurie, but down inside of her she's tough as whipcord. She'll give them a fight."

"Are you going to help?"

"She didn't ask me. She's hired a gunfighter—Pike Sides. He's mean, but he's a good man. And he will have to be. The other side are hiring gunmen—they mean to to make a fight."

They went on talking until they heard a rider coming. "That will be Freeman," Laurie said. "I want to talk to him."

Matt looked up as she rose. "Don't bring me into it. Let it be."

"I want to know what he's been doing," she said. "There were no strays over toward Strawberry, and I think he knew it. By the time he got back he was so obsessed with his own thoughts he had forgotten why he went over there."

"I know. Forget it."

The rider came into the yard, swung down, and strode

toward the door. His spurs jingled importantly. He rapped lightly, and entered when Laurie answered.

Dorset stopped abruptly when he saw Matt Coburn, and his manner changed somewhat. "I come to tell you I'm quittin', ma'am. I got me a gun job."

"I'll be sorry to see you go," Laurie said. "What do you want with a gun job, as you call it?"

"Fightin's my business," he replied brusquely. "I've hired out to Ike Fletcher. We've got some gun-fightin' to do, and he's roundin' up all the good men he can get." Dorset turned to Matt. "Surprised he hasn't asked you."

"He wouldn't dare," Matt replied quietly. "Ike Fletcher is a claim-jumper, a thief, and a murderer. If I were you, Dorset, I'd just forget the whole deal."

Dorset hooked his thumbs behind his belt. "You wouldn't talk that way to Fletcher," he said. "He's a mighty handy man with a gun." He paused. "As for that, so am I."

"I don't doubt it," Matt replied, "but Ike Fletcher is recruiting men to jump claims that belong to legal owners. In particular, he is after claims belonging to Madge Healy."

"So? If she can't hold 'em that's her lookout. She ain't nothin' but a—"

"Hold it, Dorset. Don't say another word."

There was something in Matt Coburn's tone that chilled Dorset. He hesitated. There was a time, a few days ago, when he had worked himself up to a fight with Coburn; but now as he sat here in a quiet room, looking across at Coburn, somehow dominating the silence, Dorset was uneasy.

Before he could reply, Laurie Shannon came over to him. "Here," she said, dropping coins into his hand, "now you can go, Freeman. And I'd rather you did not come back. I do not like men who hire their guns."

"What about him?" Dorset snarled, suddenly giving way to anger. His voice raised a pitch. "What about him?"

"I never hired my gun to anybody but the law," Matt

said quietly. "There's a difference, boy. Now, if you won't take my advice and leave the country, stay away from Pike Sides. He'll kill you, Dorset."

"Fat chance!" Dorset turned on his heel and strode out.

"Well, I'm short-handed," Laurie said. "I don't need many men for this outfit, but I have to have two or three."

"I know a man. He's good with a gun, but he's also a first-rate cattleman, and a good, solid man. His name is Tucker Dolan. I'll send him over." Matt paused. "He'll cover as much ground as two of Dorset, and not jingle his spurs so much."

"Madge Healy, Matt—are you in love with her?"

Startled, he looked up at Laurie, then grinned. "I scarcely know the girl. We've seen each other a bit, but I never knew her to speak to until this trip."

"That doesn't answer the question, Matt."

"No, I'm not in love with her. I don't think I'm much of a catch for any woman, and Madge has troubles of her own."

They sat for several minutes in silence. His thoughts kept straying back to Confusion. The town worried him, for he had a deep-seated aversion to destruction, and most of all, to useless vandalism. He knew what would happen over there. They would start as they had in other places with a little robbery and smashing-up, and they would end by setting fire to the town. It made no sense, for they would destroy much that was their own along with the hard work of others.

He could stop it, he knew. But stopping it would be tough and bloody. They were not men with whom you could reason, for they understood only the law of the fist and the gun. He wanted no more of that; and yet somehow he felt responsible.

"We're all responsible," he said presently to Laurie. "Law and order is a job for all of us. If we shirk it long enough we will have anarchy, and all we've built will be destroyed. It is like building a beautiful building and then turning a lot of wild animals into it and letting them go.

"This is the old war, the war of civilization against the barbarian; of peacefulness, order, and hard work against the heedless, the cruel, the destructive.

"There was a time, right at the first, here in Confusion, when a firm hand could have kept the town under control. It's gone too far for that now."

"Are you going back, Matt?" Laurie asked.

He looked up at her, smiling wryly. "It's something in me, Laurie. I know I should stay away, but I hate to see it happen. That Felton now—he doesn't like me, and I don't care much for him, but he represents something here. He's the new order in this part of the country. He stands for stability, for peace and order. You ought to latch onto him, Laurie. He'll be a big man in the country some day."

"Look who's telling me!" She laughed at him. "Matt, don't you remember? I'm wild Irish. I don't want a man who's stable and peaceful. I want a wild man." She looked right at him. "Like you, Matt."

He felt himself flushing. "Me? You couldn't do worse, Laurie. You'd never know when they'd bring me home hung over a saddle."

"No? Come back and see me after you've been to Confusion."

The town was quiet when he rode in. Again he went by the back trails, working around the arid slopes and canyons until he could come in over the top of the ridge to Discovery I. The first thing he saw was Dick Felton with a badge on his shirt.

Coburn drew up and sat his saddle, looking from Felton's face to the star. "You've got nerve. I'll give you that, Felton."

"Did you think I was afraid?"

"McGuinness wasn't afraid, either," Coburn said. "He was a brave man, and he wanted to be a good marshal. There are towns where you might run them the way you want this one run, without guns and without killing. But this isn't one of that kind."

"We will see about that," Felton said stubbornly.

"Do you know Ike Fletcher?"

Startled, Felton looked up. "What about him?"

"He's coming in. He's bringing some paid gun-hands with him, and they're going to take over Madge Healy's claims. They're here to run her out of town, out of the state, out of business. Madge Healy has Pike Sides, and I don't know who else."

Dick Felton stared down at the town, and there was a deep bitterness in him. He wanted this town to amount to something, he wanted it to become a monument to his name, a thing of pride. He resented Matt Coburn and everything he stood for, and yet at this moment he was honest enough to wish he had some of Matt's knowledge.

He looked up at the man on the horse. "What do I do? I guess it isn't enough just to walk down there with a badge."

"No, it isn't. Look, Felton, this is a specialized job. Not every man can do it—you might be one of them. I'd take a shotgun if I were you. Go down there and tell them the law, and the first one who gives you any back talk or breaks a law, just give him the butt of it in the teeth. If he reaches for a gun . . . shoot him."

"I can't do that. I want to talk to them. I want them to see that if we all work together we can have a fine town here, a prosperous one."

"Felton, law was made to protect the weak, and to save the strength of the strong. Men like Thompson and Gorman, to name just two, do not want law. They have the strength, and their strength and willingness to use it gives them power. They can take what they want. You're asking them to give up that power for something they don't want, and have never wanted. For them there is always another boom town."

"Anyway, what's so different about you?" Felton turned directly around. "If I can't run it, why can you?"

"Maybe I can't ... but I think I can, and that isn't all; *they* think I can. I have to go down there prepared to beat them at their own game, to be a little bit tougher, faster, surer. And I have the advantage that I have done it before. That helps me and handicaps them, because they know I've done it before, and some of them were even there when it happened.

"Because they know I've done it before, they won't be sure I can't do it again. That fact places the proof on *them*, and most of them don't want to stand up and be counted.

"As long as you try to face them all, you haven't a chance. You've got to single them out, you've got to make each man stand by himself, you've got to isolate them. Make each man sure that if he calls you, *he* is the one who will die, not the man beside him or behind him. Once you do that, they will break up and quit."

There was reason in the argument, Dick Felton reluctantly conceded, but having gone this far, he felt he could not retreat. All his common sense told him that he should back off now and leave the job to the professional, yet he shook off the idea, and hitched his gunbelt into place. "I can do it," he insisted, "and I am going to do it."

Matt Coburn shrugged. "Every man must go his own way, I suppose, even if it takes him to hell on the end of a six-gun."

Dan Cohan came up the street then, and crossed over to where they waited. "There's to be a meeting of the council," he said. "Olin Kingsbury is in town. He wants to talk to us."

Felton hesitated, looking toward the town. "That will wait," Cohan said. "Come on. I'll get Zeller."

He started off, then turned. "Want to drop in, Matt? If you do, come along."

Wayne Simmons, Newton Clyde, Buckwalter, Gage, and Zeller were there, as well as Cohan and Felton. Then Fife came in, keeping to the back of the room. Kingsbury, dressed in a neat dark suit, was a tall man, not over forty, and well set up. His eyes swept the group in one quick glance.

"Gentlemen, I'll come to the point at once." As he spoke, Ike Fletcher came into the room with Kendrick and Dorset. "Your town is beset with lawlessness. I have business to conduct here, and you need a marshal. I have a man, the only man who can protect you ... Big Thompson."

CHAPTER 13

As Kingsbury spoke, Big Thompson stepped into the room, thumbs hooked in his belt, his small, cruel eyes taking in the men.

"No," Felton said flatly. "Thompson has caused most of the trouble. He will not be marshal in this town."

"If you want my business—" Kingsbury began.

"I am not sure that we do." Inside, Felton was shaking, but he sounded cool. He was a man of courage, and he knew what had to be said. "I have information that you are coming in here with a crowd of hired gunmen."

Kingsbury smiled. "I do what is necessary. The town is lawless. I have property here. You are without a marshal."

"I am the marshal," Felton replied quietly. "I shall enforce the law. I shall start by saying there will be no shooting in the streets. The title of every claim that changes hands from this day on will be examined by legal authority."

Kingsbury continued to smile. "You will forgive me, Mr. Felton, if I doubt your ability to enforce that law against shooting in the streets. Thompson could enforce it. Not you."

"He will have what help he needs." Cohan spoke quietly. "And what backing he needs to enforce the law on claim titles. There will be no claim-jumping here."

The door had been left open, and now Madge Healy appeared in it, with Pike Sides. "I am glad to hear you say that, Dan," she said. "Mr. Kingsbury has some men, armed men, on the slope above the Treasure Vault. I believe they intend to move against me."

"As the heirs of your deceased husband, Miss Healy," Kingsbury said, "I believe you can look to us for protection. Those men are mine, there to protect you."

"My deceased husband," Madge said, "had no claim on my property. It was mine before I met him, and I relinquished no rights to any of it. As for protection, I have my own."

Matt Coburn had remained outside, close to an open window. He owned no property in Confusion, he held no official position, and he had no right to speak. But he could listen. At the mention of the men on the slope above the Treasure Vault, his eyes swung that way. A line of men, in skirmish formation, were moving slowly down the hill. Sure that Madge Healy would appear at the meeting, Kingsbury had chosen this time for his men to move.

Matt's own horse was up at the Discovery claim, but Clyde's horse was tethered at the hitching rail. Jerking loose the slipknot, Matt swung to the saddle. The trail to the Treasure Vault was easy; it swung around a small hill, out of sight of the men on the slope.

The horse was a fast one and it started with a lunge of speed. In scarcely more than two minutes Matt was dropping to the ground at the Treasure Vault.

There was a square stone building on the claim, a tent, and a windlass over the shaft. A man loitered at the windlass. Matt hit the ground running, letting the horse go. "How many men down there?" he demanded.

"Two . . . what's up?"

"Hell to pay. Get them up and under cover. Make it fast. Ike Fletcher's gunmen are going to try to jump the claim. They're right up the hill."

The man looked up the slope, but the men were still hidden behind a rise in the ground.

He leaned over and yelled down to the men, then grabbed hold of the rope. The first of the attackers were just coming into sight when the men emerged from the shaft.

"If you boys are fighters," Matt said, "I'll be glad of your help. Otherwise get inside and stay under cover."

"For Madge?" one of the men said. "Hell, I'll fight!" He ran for the building and the others followed.

Matt Coburn looked up the hill. The gunmen were scarcely sixty yards off, and there were at least ten of them but he had an idea there were others. He went to the stone house and stepped inside. His own rifle was on his saddle, but he took one from the rack, jacked a shell into the chamber, and picked up a box of shells from a shelf. Then he went outside again swiftly.

He came into plain view of the men, who were nearer now.

"All right, up there!" he called. "This is Matt Coburn talking. You've come far enough."

It was the name that stopped them. They could all see him standing there waiting for them, and not a man but knew his reputation.

One man spoke up. "Matt, this ain't your affair. We're workin' for Kingsbury."

"Never heard of him," Matt said contemptuously, "but I know Madge Healy, and so do fifty thousand other miners in Nevada. Suppose you take her claim away from her? Where are you boys going to go afterwards?

"You've all heard of Madge. There's fifty thousand men in Nevada who've heard her sing since she was a child. Fifty thousand who will hate your guts ... if you live through this."

There was a moment of silence, and then their leader spoke again. "Matt, you back off now. We want no trouble with you, but we've got our orders."

"All right, Smoke." Matt Coburn had placed the man.

"Here I am, and there you are. You go right ahead and follow orders."

The straggling line was motionless, each man calculating the odds. There was only one man down there, but they all knew what he could do. He could only get a few of them before they got him, but nobody wanted to be among the few who would die.

Suddenly, from behind Coburn, a voice spoke, the voice of the miner who had been at the windlass. "Don't you pay no mind to that geezer on the left, Matt. I've got him right in my sights."

From the cover of the building a second voice spoke up quickly. "An' I've got another one!"

A third voice followed. "Let 'em come, Matt. This here's goin' to be like shootin' ducks in a barrel!"

"Well, Smoke" Matt spoke almost carelessly, as though it mattered not at all to him. "That sort of evens things out, doesn't it? There's four of us, three of us under cover, and you boys all out in the open. What's it goin' to be?"

Smoke took a slow step backward. "All right, Matt," he said, "but this here's only started. We hired on for the job."

"Then you've bought yourself a ticket to Boot Hill," Matt said quietly. "All right. Get off the hillside, and make it quick. And if you want a fight you can have it, any time, any place."

Slowly, they turned around and started up the hill, but Matt Coburn knew what Smoke said was true, that this was only the beginning. Those men were not cowards. They had simply figured their chances and decided to fight another day when the odds might be changed. They were men who fought for hire, and who were hired because of their ability to get results.

A buckboard was racing along the trail, and just as Matt turned to walk back to the mine, it pulled up below. Madge Healy was there, with Pike Sides.

"You stopped them, Matt," Madge said, putting her hand on his sleeve. "You stopped them again."

"Your boys were right in there with me, Madge," he gestured toward the miners. "They stood ready to fight."

Pike stared at Matt. "You move fast, Coburn." He paused. "Was that Smoke Benton up there?"

"Uh-huh." Matt was watching Kingsbury, who was racing up in a buckboard, followed by several others.

Kingsbury drove a fine pair of bays, and they swung into the open area near the shaft and drew up in a cloud of dust. "What's going on here," he demanded.

"Mr. Kingsbury," Madge said, "you are trespassing. You are to leave this property at once, and I do not want you to come here again—for any reason whatsoever."

Kingsbury stared around, unwilling to believe his men were not in command. He started to speak when Pike Sides moved forward. "You heard the lady," he said. *"Get out!"*

Ike Fletcher, a lean man with narrow gray eyes, sat beside Kingsbury. "Pike, you're ridin' a pretty high horse there. You better step down whilst you're able."

"Turn that team," Pike said. "I'm giving you thirty seconds. I'll kill you first, Kingsbury."

Without another word the mining man swung the team and trotted them down the trail.

The afternoon was quiet. There was no sound except the usual sounds of a western town at work, and even these seemed muted. The sky was gray and lowering. Occasionally there were gusts of wind.

Dick Felton sat at the table in the building on Discovery, and waited. He wore the star, he had the gun belted on, and tonight he would take up his duties as marshal. As always, Zeller was guiding the work on the claim.

The place smelled of fresh lumber and of coffee. The door stood open; to the left was another unfinished wall of another room, still to be added. From where Felton sat he could see the street below. A stage coach had come in—they still ran only intermittently—and Wayne Simmons was talking to the driver. A dog lay in the dust in the center of the street, and whenever anyone approached he wagged his tail, as if to say, I'm comfortable—if you leave me alone, I'll leave you alone.

A few scattered horses were tied to the hitching rails. In front of the new Bon-Ton Restaurant a man sat tipped back in a wooden chair, asleep in the sun, his hat over his eyes.

It looked innocent enough. Somewhere among the tents and wagons of the more recent arrivals, a hen cackled, announcing to all that she had laid an egg.

Felton looked down the street, wondering about tonight. For the first time he was fully aware of what he was facing, and aware that he stood almost alone. Dan would back him up, so would Clyde, but they were only two against so many.

Matt Coburn loomed in the door. "How about a cup of coffee?"

"Sure. Sit down."

Matt took up the coffeepot and walked to the table with a cup, refilling Felton's, then filling his own. "You got any idea what's going to happen down here tonight?" he asked.

"I'm going to lay down the law," Felton said.

"You're going to need six sets of eyes and twelve hands," Matt said dryly. "If anybody shoots a gun, pay no attention. The chances are it will be a trick to get you into the street. You'll have to watch the dark alleyways and the roof-tops. Big Thompson may pick a fight with you, or maybe it will be Gorman or one of the others. Stay out of it. You wouldn't have a chance.

"If a fight starts over a card game," Matt went on, "stand off if you want to stop it; stand off a good distance, and watch your back. Don't back up against a wall . . . remember a forty-five cartridge will shoot through six inches of pine, and none of the walls down there are more than an inch thick.

"You'll have to move fast, and keep moving. My suggestion would be to tell them what to do and kill the first man who refuses, or moves too slow."

"I can't do that."

"Then you're a dead man."

Felton shifted in his chair. "How many bad ones are there down there?"

"Five or six who are really dangerous. A dozen more who are almost as bad, given a chance. I'd say sixty or seventy men you'll have to run out if you want a clean town."

"As many as that?"

"There are at least five hundred men around who are good, hard-working men who want no trouble with anyone, and most of them will have no trouble unless they strike it rich or show some gold around. There are at least three hundred who are all boots and shoulders. They're not bad men, but they're rough and they will fight at the drop of a hat, mostly with fists. Most of them are pretty good rough-and-tumble fighters, but they won't push a law man unless he pushes them, then they'll push back ... hard. The secret is to know who they are, ask them to lay off, or joke with them. They will only be trouble if you force them into it, but it wouldn't take much forcing ... and be careful not to hurt their pride as men. Respect them, and you won't have trouble from them. "You'll find men like that in every logging or mining camp, along every water front, and most of them are the salt of the earth. But if a green officer throws his weight around, they'll tear him to pieces. Handle them with gloves.

"It's the sixty or seventy bad ones who will give you trouble. Peggoty Gorman will shoot you from the dark, or stick a blade into you. Ike Fletcher won't kill you himself unless he's challenged."

"What about Nathan Bly?"

"Leave him alone—strictly alone. He's a killer. If you try to buck him you'll have to kill him, and that will take some doing. On the other hand, Bly won't go looking for trouble ... and in time he'll drift to another town."

They were silent for a time, watching the street. The dog sat up, scratched, and trotted away. A man came out of the Bon-Ton and started to sweep off the walk. The sound of double-jacks on steel drills came from several quarters as the miners worked. There was the sound of driving nails, of a saw ... a horse whinnied.

Madge Healy came out of the one-room shack that was the stage station, shading her eyes as she looked up toward Discovery. Matt wondered about her, as he had many times in the past few days. She was all woman, that one, and strikingly attractive, but she was bucking almost impossible odds in taking on Willard & Kingsbury.

Their machinations had affected the life of more than one mining camp. They moved in, using the law when it served them, using force when necessary, but usually they tried to take over the law and use it with legal force to accomplish their ends. Not many of the miners had the money to fight them in the courts, but Kingsbury rarely let it come to that. He was a man of violence who employed men of violence. Matt Coburn had never had occasion to buck them before.

A man strolled out of a saloon now and stood on the walk. From the distance it was hard to be sure, but that affected walk looked like the style of Freeman Dorset. With him was another man ... probably Kendrick, formerly of the Harry Meadows' outfit.

Felton suddenly looked over at Matt. "Why are you giving me all this advice? I've never liked you, and you've had no reason to like me."

"I don't pay much attention to whether people like me or not. In my business you get over being thin-skinned. I like what you want to do here, and I am against them." He gestured toward the town. "I suppose that basically we want the same things. No lawman ever gets rich. We suffer and we die, and usually we die young, and there's precious little thanks for us when we go. Yet without us this country could never survive and grow, without us you could never have the town you're wanting.

"If you're going to have peace rather than violence, both sides have got to want it. One side alone can't make peace. You cannot go down there and talk the law and the rights of the public to men who can only profit by breaking the law. They just aren't going to listen."

"What do you think will happen when I go down there tonight?" Felton asked.

"Tonight, or maybe tomorrow night, they will try to kill you. If you're lucky you might get away with a wound. Dan Cohan and Newt Clyde will try to back you up, and the boys down there will know it. You may get one or both of them killed, too."

"And then?"

"They'll run wild. They'll tear the town apart, they'll burn, and they'll kill, and then there won't be any reason for staying on, so they'll drift. And that will be the end of your town. A few of the mines may still be worked, and some ore shipped to one of the mills, but five years from now the town will be dead, and in time even its name will be forgotten."

"What about the buildings?"

"Some will be carried away in pieces, some used by the miners who stay on, some will be broken up for firewood. After a few years there will only be a few holes in the mountainside and the fallen walls of what stone buildings there are. I have seen it happen before.

"The trouble with most folks coming out here is that they've been protected so long they're no longer even conscious of it. Back where they come from there are rules and laws, curbstones and sidewalks, and policemen to handle violence. The result is that violence is no longer real for them; it is something you read about but that never happens to you."

Matt paused for a moment, and went on. "You're a brave man, Felton, but you're a stubborn one. You will go down there tonight and get somebody killed. The only rule those men understand is force, or the threat of force.... Well, there ... I've talked too much."

Felton was silent. Despite his stubbornness, he had the feeling that what Matt Coburn had said was the truth. He frowned ... he did not want to die, and he did not want anyone else to die because of his actions. But he made up his mind.

He stood up. "I'm going down there and talk to them," he said. "I'm going to tell them what kind of a town we want—what kind of a town we'll have if they will cooperate."

Matt smiled at him. "Felton, that's like asking a tiger to take up grazing with the sheep. It's against their nature. But you can try it."

"I won't wear a gun," Felton said. He unbuckled his belt. "I'll go down there and reason with them."

Leaving his gunbelt on the table, he strode to the door and went out. Matt drank the last of his coffee. He sat there for a few minutes more, watching the sunlight as it fell through the door.

He suddenly found himself thinking of Laurie Shannon, and how the sunlight had fallen through the flowered curtains at her windows; he remembered the smell of coffee and the quiet, pleasant room. She had a gift, that one, for realizing comfort, a feeling of security and rest.

He got up, hitched his gunbelt into place, and walked to the door. He stared down at the town, and at the bleak hills, so recently untouched by man but now ripped and torn by the feverish search for gold.

There was no beauty in the town. There was no tree, no flower, no shrub except for the gray-green drouth-resistant plants of the desert. Only two of the buildings had been painted, most were of new lumber. Only a few had boardwalks in front of them.

He did not want this town for his own. He did not want to know it better, and he did not want to remain here. The amateurs were trying to do a job that needed a professional. He knew that some of Felton's dislike for him had abated, and he felt that the young man was perhaps half convinced by what he had said, but he had little hope for him or for the town. He knew what he himself could do—with a bit of luck—but he had no desire to do it.

He found himself liking Felton. The man was an idealist, but he was a solid young man with a future—if he survived Confusion.

He went outside, saddled his horse, and led it across to the stage station.

Dick Felton was walking down the street alone. Madge Healy was standing in the door, watching him go. She looked at Matt. "Are you going to help him, Matt"

"No."

"You helped me."

"That was different. You're a woman, and alone. No, Felton wants no help. He's got his own ideas, and he has to go his own way."

"They'll kill him, Matt. Or maybe worse ... they'll break him."

He stood beside her, thinking that she probably had seen even more of such towns than he had. For all the years since she was a small child she had been dancing and singing in the boom towns, in lonely camps ... everywhere.

"What's going to happen, Matt?" she asked.

He shrugged. "We've got two things going here: anarchy in the camp, and an organization working against you. They'll feed on each other. Once the town starts to come apart at the seams, Kingsbury and Fletcher will move against you."

He considered for a moment. "If I were you, I'd keep Pike at the claim, and whatever power you have. Whatever happens will start tonight."

He saw that Felton had gone into the Main Chance Saloon.

CHAPTER 14

"Matt, what about you?" Madge looked searchingly into his eyes. "When this is over, what are you going to do?"

"I'm getting a ranch. I'm going to settle down and stay put."

She smiled. "Do you think you can? Do you think they will let you? Or that you will let yourself? We're two of a kind, Matt, and we've both been as homeless as a pair of tumbleweeds. That's why I was so easy to convince when Scollard started talking to me about a home and lace curtains. I was lonely, Matt, lonely as only you could understand. I don't think that way down deep I believed him for a minute, but I believed in what he was telling me because I wanted to so desperately."

Their eyes were on the door of the Main Chance. Dick Felton had not come out yet, but a moment later he did emerge and walked on down the street, stopping in stores, saloons, restaurants, and the gambling tents. In each place he stayed only a few minutes. When he had visited every public place, he walked back up the hill to Discovery and went into the stone building.

It was Sturdevant Fife who came up the hill to explain. Wayne Simmons, Clyde, Cohan, and Zeller were there to listen. "He's quite a speaker, that boy. Ever' place he went, he gave them a spiel on what a fine town

128

this was going to be; about the schools, the churches, and all, and the need for teamwork to make it thataway. I'd say he made him a good talk."

"What kind of response did he get?" Simmons asked skeptically.

Fife shrugged. "Well," he said, "it reminded me of some politicians I've knowed, time to time. Those who were goin' to vote for them anyway needed no convincing. You might say their response was downright enthusiastic. Then there was the other lot who wouldn't vote for him a-tall, and they just listened. I'd say he put hisself on record, and he made a good try."

There was silence in the room, and then Cohan said, "We'd better help him. We'd better go down there armed and ready."

"You'd be wasting your time, Dan," Simmons said, "and you know it. This town has gone too far without the law. They'd see us coming and there'd be an ambush." Simmons sat down behind his desk. "Dick wants to play this hand alone, and as far as I'm concerned, he can play it."

Zeller shifted his heavy body, and his chair creaked. "Vat aboudt Coburn? Su'bose ve hire him our ownselfs?"

"He won't take it." Fife said flatly. "Only if you give him a free hand. And he'll run it with a gun."

"I t'ink dere iss no udder vay," Zeller said calmly.

Tucker Dolan rode into the yard at the Rafter LS and swung down from his horse. He had been punching cows for Laurie Shannon for several days, and he liked it.

Laurie stepped to the door. "Come in, Tucker. Your supper will get cold."

"Ma'am," Dolan hesitated, then went on, "I ain't been with you long, but I'd admire to have a couple of days off."

"What is it?"

"Well, ma'am, it's Matt Coburn. Matt's goin' to be wearin' the badge over at Confusion by daylight tomorrow. I've got a feelin' he may need help."

"He's been saying he would never wear a badge again, not for anybody."

"It's Felton, ma'am. That young feller who owns part of Discovery. I run into a traveler today, a man headed for Hamilton, Nevada. He told me that Felton's going to wear the badge tonight. That means he ain't goin' to wear it long, and when he goes down the whole town of Confusion is goin' to go with him. The only man who could stop it is Matt, so he'll step in. No matter what he says, he's a man who rises to trouble. An' ma'am, he's a-goin' to need all the help he can get."

Laurie turned and spoke over her shoulder. "Did you hear that, Joss?"

"I heerd, an' I reckon he's right. You mind if I ride along, too?"

"We'll all go." Laurie spoke quietly. "I can handle a rifle as well as most men, better than some. I will just ride along."

"Now see here, ma'am—" Joss started to protest.

"Don't waste our time. I am going, too. Joss, will you saddle some horses while Tucker eats?"

Confusion came slowly to life on this night. There were no random shots, fired in careless exuberance by some drunken miner, and the street was less crowded than on recent nights.

A piano in the Main Chance began to play, followed by a music box in one of the gambling tents. A drifting cowboy, travel-stained and weary, rode in at sundown. He swung down, eased the girth on his saddle, and tied his horse.

Pausing on the street, he rolled and lit a cigarette, looking uneasily around. Another music box, in the Bucket of Blood, began to jangle. The cowboy looked down the street, then he went back to his horse and tightened the cinch, hesitated, and went into a counter lunch just off the street. A few men were gathering at the Main Chance, a few more at the Bucket.

Madge Healy had gone to her claim for a last check

before nightfall. She had rented a cabin from a miner who had squatted on the hillside not far back of the stage office, and she would go back there to sleep. But when she returned from the claim she prepared a small meal for herself, and sat down to wait. When she poured her coffee the brush of evening was painting the eastern hills with mauve and shadow, with here and there a streak of vivid light along the crests of the ridges.

But Madge Healy was not thinking of the sunset, nor of the events in the hours to come. She was thinking of Matt Coburn. Her common sense told her he was a man going nowhere but to his death in some dusty street; yet from the first time she had seen him, when she was only a child and he had not known who she was, she had felt strangely drawn to him. He would not remember that meeting, with a child whom he touched for a moment on the shoulder, and to whom he had spoken gently.

She had seen him several times since then, and never without excitement. That he was going nowhere meant nothing to her; she herself had done well in these past few years, better than anyone knew or was likely to know. That was one thing her aunt had done for her: she had taught her to think for herself and plan for herself, but now she had it and here she was, fighting a man's fight against men, when all she wanted was a home and a man ... Matt Coburn.

He was the only man she had ever known who made her feel protected. He made her feel safe, secure. And the feeling was strange to her.

From her window she could see the house on Discovery, so she saw Dick Felton when he came out into the street. He always dressed well, and he was dressed with exceptional care tonight. And he wore a gun.

"I hope they don't make you use it," she said aloud.

How many such towns had she seen? From the Mother Lode country of California to the Comstock in Nevada, and to Montana, Utah, Idaho, Colorado, and Arizona. She had been performing for six years before she ever saw the inside of a theatre. She was not the only one, of course. Lotta Crabtree had begun the same way, dancing on stumps or barrel-tops, on planks or boxes—anywhere at all. Most of the homesick men hadn't seen a child in so long they would have paid just to see her, even if she had not performed ... and at first she must have been pretty bad.

Lights came on in the town now as she sat there, and the sounds picked up, yet they seemed somehow muted, for the town was waiting, crouching like a beast in its lair.

Dick Felton started down the street. There was no sign of Matt Coburn.

Dan Cohan walked outside the stage station with Simmons and Clyde. He carried a shotgun in the hollow of his arm.

"Don't do it, Dan," Simmons warned. "There's no use you both getting killed. Felton might just swing it."

"You know he won't. As for me. I came west with him. We went partners in this deal, and I'm a partner all the way."

"They know you, Dan. They'll expect you, be sure of that. Whatever it is they've planned for tonight, they'll be ready for you too."

Madge Healy came up and stopped in the street close to Dan Cohan. "Where's Matt?" she asked.

"I haven't seen him."

Newt Clyde pointed toward the back of Jim Gage's place. His wagon was drawn up there, half loaded with goods. "He's pullin' out," Clyde said. "Well, there it is, boys. I never knew Gage to miss. When he leaves, the town is finished."

"Not this town." Cohan was adamant. "He's goin' to be wrong this time."

Simmons stood by the door. "I wonder where Matt is. I'm going to lock up. If the place starts to burn, this office might escape the fire, being off by itself the way it is."

Sturdevant Fife nodded toward the street. "Ain't one

of Fletcher's killers in sight. He's pulled 'em all off the street."

Tucker Dolan, still several miles out of town, had called it right. Matt Coburn could not stay out of it. When a town was in bad trouble, he was like an old fire horse. He had to be there. Despite the fact that there had been antagonism between Felton and himself, he respected the man too much to let him go alone into the hell that lay before him. Also, during their last talk Felton had been less assertive, more willing to listen.

Matt Coburn had a feeling that Felton would have liked to back up, but simply did not know how. He had stated his case, and was going to follow through if it killed him—and it probably would. So Matt Coburn had quietly disappeared.

This was an old trick, and one he had learned long ago. It was a handy thing to do sometimes, for there was much a good officer of the law should not notice. Many little difficulties settled themselves if ignored, but if pushed they explode into real trouble. Matt had learned to disappear when such things developed.

He studied a town like a chessboard. He knew where every alley led, where back fences might get in the way, whether back doors were locked or unlocked. He had never entered a town in the past seven or eight years without mentally scouting it. Within a few hours after his arrival he could tell you what doors and windows covered what particular portions of the street.

He knew every possible firing point, every bit of cover, every means of getting quickly from one place in the town to another. He knew every point where he might be subjected to a cross-fire. And now he had an idea of what would happen when Felton went down into the town.

At first, all would be quiet, to lull him into a feeling of security. Then there would be a disturbance, a fight faked for his benefit, or something requiring his attention. When Felton arrived, they would crowd around, pushing closer and closer until he could no longer move, or even draw a gun. Then they would have his guns, and would begin to bait him, pushing, shoving, getting more and more violent until it ended in a killing or maiming.

Or they might choose to fake a shooting in the street, and when he came to stop it, they would open fire from concealment and simply kill him. That would be Ike Fletcher's way. Big Thompson, a rowdy at heart, would incline toward the other, rowdy way of doing things.

There were dozens of ways of killing a man or of breaking him down to size, and Matt Coburn knew them all. And so it was that a few hours before darkness settled, Matt had quietly dropped from sight.

Behind the Bon-Ton Restaurant the hillside curved away from the narrow gulch started by that long-dead coyote and merged with the wash that lay at the foot of the slope. Scattered on the hillside were slabs of rock, and higher up were a few cabins, dugouts, and tents. Among the rock slabs Matt had noticed one place that offered shelter from observation.

He had eaten a meal of beef and chili and enjoyed several cups of coffee, and after that he had walked out back and seated himself on a rock in the sun. After a while he stood up, idly checked a few chunks of float picked up from the hillside, and then he disappeared into his chosen place of concealment. One moment he had been idling along the hillside, the next he was gone. He felt that he had not been seen, and he settled back to rest.

Dusk had come, and the town awakened slowly and cautiously to its night life. In the darkness on the hillside, Matt Coburn came out of hiding. He hitched his guns into place, one in its holster, the other in his waistband. Then he went down to the back of the Bon-Ton and walked along the dark alleyway that led to the street. He paused there, still in the darkness, watching the street.

He knew at that moment that he wanted to go away. He wanted to turn around, go back up the hill to his horse, saddle up, and ride away—he did not care where.

But in the back of his mind there was the memory of a ranch house with curtained windows and the sunlight falling across the floor, the memory of the smell of coffee and the sense of quiet.

Was it really that he wanted? Or was he, like Madge Healy, just trying to escape from what he was and what he had been? Was it the warmth and comfort of a home he wanted, or was it the cool stillness of the high, pine-covered plateaus? And would he be willing to remain where there was peace, or would he return always to these new towns peopled by tough, brawling men who could build towns, but who carried within themselves their own destruction? Perhaps wherever he was, he would have to be the lawman, the preserver of the peace.

He shook himself. He was thinking too much. This was no time for thinking. That came before, or it came after; now was a time for feeling, for sensing—and for action, if need be.

He could hear footsteps, and knew it was Dick Felton.

Outside the Bucket of Blood a man struck a match to light a cigarette ... or was it a signal? At the Main Chance a man strolled through the swinging doors and stopped on the edge of the walk . . . a momentary glimpse as he passed through the doors showed that it was Kid Curtis.

A moment later Matt realized that the man who had lighted the cigarette was Parsons, who had been at the stage station with Tucker Dolan. Matt Coburn eased himself further toward the street, but he was still in the shadows. Dick Felton had gone into the Bon-Ton. Another man came out and leaned against the awning post. It was Peggoty Gorman.

This was it, then. The thing Matt did not know was their plan of action. He had an idea there would be a fake shooting, and when Felton came to interfere they would kill him with a "stray" bullet. If it happened that way there could be no repercussions from Felton's partners or friends.

These men were the lawless, rowdy element that centered around Thompson, not the more cool-headed hired gunmen Ike Fletcher would have. Fletcher would be planning to move when trouble started in town. With everybody busy there, he could strike quick and hard against Madge Healy's claims.

Medley, the gunman who worked partners with Parsons, was nowhere in sight, but he would be involved if Parsons was, so he must be around somewhere, in concealment.

Suddenly, the saloon doors were pushed open and Dick Felton stepped out on the boardwalk. Matt Coburn took a careful step closer to the street, and slipped the thong from his gun.

Nobody moved. The street, lighted from nearby doors and windows, was quiet. Kid Curtis lounged nearby. Peggoty Gorman leaned against the awning post near Felton. Parsons was across the street.

A man was on each side of Felton, a man across the street, but nobody moving, not a word being spoken.

CHAPTER 15

Dick Felton hesitated. He must have sensed a trap, for these men were known to him as troublemakers, yet all they were doing was just standing there.

The swinging doors moved again, and two more men came out. They stopped right behind Felton.

Matt was on the edge of the street now, but he was still hidden in the shadow, close against a building.

One of them spoke. "Howdy, Mr. Marshal." That was Peg Gorman. "You bringin' the law to Confusion?"

"I am." Felton's voice was calm. "And it's about time."

"I like that. A public-spirited citizen. We boys know how to appreciate a public-spirited citizen, don't we, boys?"

"Sure do," came from one of the men behind Felton. "That's why we brung a bottle along. Seems to us a public-spirited citizen should be almighty dry right now. Spirits to the spirited, ain't that what we say, boys?"

"A drink," Gorman said. "We'll all have a drink. You'll drink with us, won't you, Marshal?"

"You boys have the drink. I'll wait until I'm off duty."

"We take that unkindly, Mr. Marshal. You figure you're too good to drink with us boys? Course, we ain't big tall lawmen, and we don't own any fancy minin'

137

claims, but we're good boys and we figured you'd have a drink with us. After all, what's one little snort?"

Matt Coburn could understand the hesitation in Felton's mind. Should he, or shouldn't he? Were they really out to make trouble, or could he by this small gesture win their cooperation?

"Sorry." Felton even made his voice sound as if he meant it. "Not while I'm on duty. You boys come up and see me tomorrow, and I'll break out a bottle. Now I've got to get along."

"Wait."

Felton looked at Gorman. Across the street, Parsons stepped off the walk. Felton heard Kid Curtis stirring behind him.

Matt knew Felton was thinking: *What should I do?* But it was already too late for thinking; he should be moving.

"Now, you wouldn't walk out on us, would you, Marshal?" Gorman's tone was sly, teasing. "Ain't often we get your comp'ny down here. I figure we should make the most of it."

"I think he should drink with us," Curtis said flatly. "I think that's only fair." He put his hand on Felton's shoulder, and Felton turned sharply to push it off.

"Kind of touchy, ain't you, Marshal? You too good for us boys?"

"This has gone far enough." Felton spoke sternly. "Back off now!"

Somebody laughed. Then Curtis said. "He's right, Peg," and he pushed Peggoty back on his heels. "Leave him alone. This here town needs a good marshal."

"You leave me alone!" Gorman retorted, and he shoved Curtis back, but somehow he shoved him against Felton, and Felton staggered, falling against the two men behind him. One grabbed his right arm and belt, the other his gun. Then they shoved him away and the others backed off, forming a circle around him.

Disarmed and trapped, Felton stood in their midst, and he knew they were going to destroy him.

At that instant, Dan Cohan appeared in the street. He held his shotgun, and he spoke loud and clear. "All right, boys, back off from him now or I'll kill you!"

A gunshot rolled a smashing reverberation against the walls, and Cohan fell. So that was where Medley was . . . on the roof.

Immediately other men began to appear from doors, edging toward the street. "Come on, boys!" Curtis yelled. "We got us a marshal! Let's see how he'd look in tar an' feathers!"

Matt Coburn was still in the shadow, but suddenly his voice sounded, sharp and clear to all. "Peg Gorman! This is Matt Coburn! Drop your gunbelt, and get back against the building . . . Gorman, you've got thirty seconds to get rid of that belt!"

A split second of hesitation, and Gorman stripped the belt and dropped it. "You too, Curtis! Fast! The rest of you get off the street!"

They couldn't see him. They knew about where he was, but there was no clear target, and everybody knew about Matt Coburn . . . he would kill.

The crowd that had been gathering began disappearing. Curtis gingerly unfastened his gunbelt and let it drop.

"Medley! Get off that roof!" Matt called. "Don't make me come up there after you! And throw down your gun!"

Parsons alone had not moved. He was staring hard into the shadows. "Coburn, you ain't got me bluff—"

Coburn's gun stabbed flame and the man staggered back and went down. Parsons made a feeble effort to rise, but he fell back.

Medley was down in the street now. "I'll kill you for that, Coburn!" he shouted.

"All right, Med! Pick up your gun. You can have your chance right now. Go ahead . . . pick it up!"

"I'll be damned if—!"

"Pick it up, Med! Pick it up, or I'll shoot you where you stand!"

Medley hesitated, then he dived for his gun. There was no shot. He grasped the gun, got slowly to his feet.

Coolly, Matt Coburn stepped into view. "All right, Med. If you want to kill me, here I am. You've got your chance."

Unbelievingly, Medley stared at him. He held the gun half raised. Matt Coburn also held his. Medley began to sweat. Here it was, his chance to kill Coburn.

"Go ahead, Medley. You asked for it. Shoot, or drop that gun. But if you drop it, you ride out of town before sunrise, or I'll shoot you on sight."

Medley started to lift the gun, looking across at Coburn, who stood waiting, his own gun half lifted, an almost amused smile on his face. Abruptly, Medley dropped his gun and, turning on his heel, walked from the street.

"Felton, get your gun from that man," Matt said, "and go over and check on Dan."

Moving carefully so as to keep out of Coburn's line of fire, Felton retrieved his gun, and went to Dan.

Matt Coburn waved the others together with his pistol. "I'm not going to give any orders," he said quietly, "but from now on I'm running this town. If any of you have any doubts about what that means, ask Mr. Parsons yonder.

"If you boys want to work, you file claims or get jobs. Otherwise . . . move. Mr. Felton and the council want a clean town and I'm going to give it to them. Now, scatter out and drift . . . if I see any of you on the street tonight you'd better see me first. I won't give any warnings."

Slowly, they filed from the street. During all of this, Matt had moved with care so as to offer no chance to a hidden marksman, and when the men had gone he simply stepped back into the shadows and worked his way along the street, noting whoever was visible in the saloons as he passed them.

Half an hour later he was back in the stage office at the head of the street. "All right," he said. "I didn't want the job, but Felton was too good a man to have that happen to him. If you want me to wear the badge I'll do it . . . until your town has been cleaned up."

"You'd better have some deputies," Clyde said.

"No, I'll handle it alone."

He took the badge, and listened to them telling him that Dan Cohan was not badly hurt. The bullet had been slightly deflected by a button on his shirt and had skidded upward, ripping a long gash in his chest and shoulder and knocking him down. For a moment he had been stunned, unable to move.

Matt Coburn awoke before daylight with a bad taste in his mouth. Swinging his feet to the floor, he got up and padded across the room the storekeeper Gage had offered him. He stared into the mirror without pleasure, and then dressed and shaved.

As he shaved, he listened to the sounds of the town. They told him all was normal. He had heard a screen door open and close, a windlass squeaking and groaning. Occasionally a rooster crowed.

When he was dressed he looked around the room until he found a tablet that Gage had been using to total orders, and sitting down he began to write. When he had filled two pages, he got up, found some tacks and a hammer, and went outside.

The street was empty. The gray of early morning hung over it, while here and there up on the hillside a lamp or lantern still burned. Back of Buckwalter's he found some scrap lumber and some nails. He tacked a board to a post, and carried it right into the middle of the street in front of the Bon-Ton, and there he drove the sharpened end of the post into the ground. When it was up, he tacked on the two sheets on which he had written.

In the Bon-Ton Newt Clyde was already at breakfast, and when Matt came in he gestured toward the post outside. "What's that?"

"You tell Wayne he's going to have to put on a couple

of extra stages for a few days. If he hasn't got the stages, tell him to use freight wagons—anything."

Clyde looked at him curiously. "Heard you pulled Dick out of a hole last night. I thought you two didn't like each other."

"He doesn't like me," Matt said. "I've nothing against him. I figure he's a pretty good man ... too good to lose to that bunch."

"Did you have to kill Parsons?"

"If I hadn't killed him I'd have had to kill Medley, and maybe some others. Parsons has been buckin for it for years."

When Newt Clyde finished his coffee he got up and went out to read the sign. Several others were already there.

NOTICE

To Thieves, Murderers, and Short-card Artists;
You are no longer welcome in Confusion.
Those listed below can get out or shoot it out,
and start any time they are ready.

There followed a list of seventy names. The name signed to the notice was simply: MATT.

Newt Clyde whistled softly. A man behind him said to his companion, "Come on, let's get loaded up."

"What's the matter?" the other man sneered. "You scared?"

"Mister, have you ever seen the way Matt Coburn cleans up a town?"

Matt came out of the Bon-Ton, glanced up and down the street, then crossed over, walking quickly, eyes alert, ears taking in every sound. He stopped before the Nugget, where Big Kate was standing. "How are you going to run it, Kate?"

"It's your town, Matt. I'll run it clean."

"Thanks, Kate. If you have any trouble, call on me."

"If I have any trouble"—Kate put her big fists on her hips—"I'll handle it myself."

At the next door down the street, he paused again. This was Rocking-Chair Emma's, and the woman came out. She had once been slim and attractive; now she was slat-thin and nail-hard. "Em, we understand each other. You give cause for one complaint, and you get out."

"There's men around wouldn't want to see me go," she said with a sneer. "What would you do about that?"

"You've been told, Em. And you'll find their names out there"—he indicated the sign—"so they know what they can do."

"Thompson will kill you, Matt. Big Thompson will wipe the earth with you!"

He grinned at her. "Em, the one thing we know about life is that we'll never get out of it alive. Thompson's name is on the list."

Slanting Annie heard the talk and came to the door. "What is it, Matt?"

"The town's on notice, Annie. You've always run a straight place. Stay on as long as you like."

He went from place to place. At the Bucket of Blood, he stepped inside and looked around. Kid Curtis was there, and behind the bar was Tobe Burnside, a Barbary Coast bully. "Check the list," he told them. "Your names are posted."

Burnside smiled and leaned his ponderous forearms on the bar. "I'm going to wait, Coburn. I'm going to wait until Thompson gets through with you."

"You do that, Tobe. But when I'm through with Thompson you'd better hit the street running. If you wait that long you won't be taking anything with you but a little hide . . . and not much of that."

Matt started up the street to where Wayne Simmons, Clyde, and Zeller were waiting. Suddenly a voice sounded behind him. It was Nathan Bly.

Matt turned slowly. Bly was standing in the center of the walk, staring at him. All along the street, people had stopped to watch.

Bly indicated the sign with a jerk of his head. "My

name's not on the list. Why?" His pale blue eyes staring into Matt's he waited.

"Because you're a gentleman, Nate. You're a damned good man with cards, but you have your proper pride. You've never cheated anybody in your life."

Nathan Bly's face showed nothing, but when he spoke there was a faint surprise in his tone. "You called me a gentleman, Matt."

"Well, aren't you? Nate, I've seen you around for six or seven years. I never knew you to be anything else. You go ahead and run your place, but don't shoot anybody unless you have to." Abruptly, he turned and walked back up the street toward the waiting men.

Nathan Bly went back to his gambling tent and stepped inside. The gamblers were waiting, watching him. "You boys heard that," he said harshly, "so you know what to do. Any man who tries any fancy stuff will answer to me, d'you hear? We run it straight, we run it honest."

Dan Cort got up from behind his table. "I quit," he said coldly. "I'll start my own house. Right here in town."

"You do that," Nathan replied shortly.

"As for Matt Coburn," Cort said, "I've never seen any of his graveyards."

Nathan Bly smiled. "You will, Cort. You will!"

Dan Cort hitched his gun into place, then slipped on his coat. "You watch this!" he said. "Just watch!"

He stepped out on the street, Matt Coburn was standing talking to Clyde and Simmons. Cort stepped into the middle of the street. "Matt! *Matt Coburn!*"

Coburn turned as the men he'd been talking to broke for shelter. As he turned, Dan Cort drew and fired. It was a blazingly fast draw, and Cort fired instantly.

The bullet kicked up dirt six feet in front of Coburn, and the second bullet scattered splinters from the boardwalk near Matt's knee.

Matt had drawn easily, almost casually. Now he fired.

Dan Cort took a slow step forward, his knees buckled and he fell.

Inside the gambling tent Nathan Bly looked over at his swamper. "Mixter, get somebody to help you and dig Dan a grave, will you? Put a marker on it that reads: *He drew against Matt Coburn.*"

Clyde came out of his office, his face pale. "That was close!" he said.

Coburn shrugged. "He was too anxious to get his gun out. The fast draw is only part of it. You have to make the first shot count."

"Now what?" Clyde asked.

Matt smiled. "I'm going to get Big Thompson," he said quietly. "I want him to read that sign. And give me that shotgun, will you? I don't want him to try to draw on me until I'm through saying what I've got to say."

Taking the shotgun, Matt went between two buildings and around another, approaching Thompson's cabin from the corner on the side where there was no window. He walked up to the door, drew back his foot, and kicked hard at the lock. The flimsy door flew open and Matt stepped in quickly, double-barreled shotgun in his right hand.

Peggoty Gorman was sitting up in bed, blinking. Big Thompson rolled up to one elbow, astonished and unbelieving.

"All right, Thompson! Roll out and put on your pants!"

"What is this?" Big Thompson's eyes found the badge on Coburn's shirt. "Come to that, has it? I been waitin' for it."

Matt Coburn moved suddenly, holding the sawed-off shotgun in his right hand. He grabbed the flimsy cot with his left hand, and with one powerful jerk upward he dumped Thompson on the floor.

The big man scrambled for an instant, and lunged to his feet. Matt took a step back, the shotgun fixed on Thompson's belly. "That's better. Glad you sleep in your socks, Thompson, come on."

"Where to?"

"Just down in the street. You, too, Peggoty. And if you boys want to get funny, just try it and I'll cut you in two."

Thompson stared at him. "You give me an even break, an' I'll cut you down."

"That's what Dan Cort thought. He got his break."

"Cort?" Cort was a known friend of Thompson's. They had been in Silver Reef together.

"He's dead," Matt said.

"It's like I tried to tell you, Big," Gorman said. "You were too drunk to listen. He killed Parsons last night."

Thompson walked out of the door, and Gorman followed. As two dozen people watched, Matt Coburn marched them to the center of the street. There at least fifty men had already collected, staring at the sign.

"Back up, boys," Coburn said to them pleasantly. "I want these two chickens to read the notice. Then we'll let them hunt a new roost."

Clyde was there, and Simmons, Buckwalter, and Zeller, and now Dick Felton. Three of them had rifles, two were armed with shotguns.

Big Thompson stared at the list, then looked around at Matt Coburn. "Get out or shoot it out, eh? An' me without a gun?"

Matt Coburn unbuckled his belt, removed the gun from his waistband, and handed them to Felton. "You boys see that we're not interrupted, will you? Thompson's brag is that he can break any man with his hands. Maybe he's right."

"You bet I'm—"

Matt feinted a right and stabbed a quick left to Big Thompson's mouth. It was unexpected and jarring. Big shook his head and put the back of a hand to his mouth, to find blood on it. He leaped at Matt, wanting to get his hands on him, and expecting him to move away. Instead, Matt stepped inside one of the huge arms and smashed short, wicked punches to the belly.

They caught Thompson coming in, and he grunted

with the impact of the blows. Then Matt whipped a right uppercut to the chin that snapped Thompson's head back, hard.

But Thompson was old in the rough game of fighting. He had taken punches before. He pulled his head down and rolled his huge weight against Coburn. Matt hooked hard to the belly, caught a jarring blow to the jaw that staggered him, and a back-hand blow to the cheek-bone that sent him reeling against the water trough.

Thompson rushed to get close, punching hard with both hands. Matt swung a left to the belly as the big man came in, but he caught two more high hard ones to the head. He ducked, smashed upward with the top of his head against Thompson's chin, then stamped on his instep.

The big man howled with pain and backed off. For a moment they circled.

"I'm going to kill you, Coburn! I'm goin' to wreck you good."

Thompson was wary now, but he was a powerful man, and he knew what he could do. He had killed a man with his fists before this.

CHAPTER 16

Matt Coburn was aware that the crowd had increased. He was aware that the sun was higher, and that it had grown warmer. All this he knew, but in a secondary way. The one fact that stood out now was that he had underestimated Big Thompson.

He had known that he was strong. He had expected him to be a tough fighter, but he had not expected such a brute of strength and fury as now faced him.

They circled each other warily. Matt was a big man himself, although sixty pounds lighter than Thompson. He had done his share of fighting and brawling, and he had learned long since that in most cases the very big man, having been large even as a boy, had never had to fight as much as a smaller man had, and so had never developed the fighting skill or ferocity a smaller man must need to develop to survive. But this was not true of Thompson. The big man was not only big, not only strong—he was also a real fighter.

Instinctively, Matt had gone for the body. His old policy had always been to "get them where they live." Many a man can take them on the chin, but very few have their stomach muscles developed to the point where they are impervious to blows. Moreover, Matt knew that even the tough ones cannot stand up to much battering in the mid-section.

Thompson moved in. He not only had big fists, but somewhere, at one time or another, he had done some boxing.

Coburn circled, and Thompson feinted suddenly and threw a whistling right hand to the head, but Coburn went under it, smashing a right to the ribs that made the big man gasp. Then Thompson grabbed him, heaving him off his feet and clasping both hands against Coburn's sides in a crushing grasp. One arm free, Matt hooked again and again to Big Thompson's face, smashing him with short, wicked blows as the bigger man bent him back and back. Excruciating pain caught Coburn in the back, and suddenly he kicked up with both feet, tumbling both of them to the ground. The fall broke Thompson's hold and Coburn rolled free.

He was the first on his feet and he caught Thompson in the mouth with a roundhouse swing as the bigger man was getting up. The blow dropped Thompson to his knees, and started the blood flowing from his mouth.

Coburn backed off, wanting to catch his wind. Thompson got to his feet, his face twisted with rage. In a half-crouch, he came toward Matt, who waited. Suddenly Matt stepped in, smashing a left jab to the mouth and a right to the chin. Both blows stuck solidly, but Thompson merely bowed his head and drove in, butting Coburn in the chest.

Knocked off balance, Matt went down, and Thompson leaped high to come down on him with both feet. Twisting sharply away, Matt kicked out, missed, kicked again as Big Thompson started for him again. The kick caught Thompson on the knee, stopping him momentarily.

Matt scrambled to all fours and drove at Thompson with a smashing tackle. Thompson side-stepped, and when Matt sprawled on the ground he leaped astride him.

But quick as Big Thompson was, Matt rolled over and

met his leap with raised knees and a fierce shove, throwing Thompson to the ground. Both men came up fast and lunged at each other, swinging hard. Matt felt jarring blows to his head, and one that smashed into his ribs with knifing pain, and then he connected with a right that split Thompson's cheekbone, showering him with blood.

Thompson put his head down and plowed in, but Matt rolled away from the rush, smashing a hard one to the ribs, and when Thompson straightened, Matt smashed another hard right to the mouth. Thompson grabbed at him, ripped his shirt, then caught his arm and jerked him into a clinch. Matt dropped his head to Thompson's shoulder in time, and spreading his legs, stuck at his belly with short, vicious blows.

They broke apart and stood for an instant, gasping and bloody, and then with one accord they moved in quickly. But instantly Matt changed tactics. Grasping one of the extended arms, he turned and threw Thompson with a rolling hip-lock. The big man went down hard, and for an instant he lay as if stunned.

Matt moved back, hands working, waiting for Thompson to get up. He got up slowly, and Matt walked in, suddenly avid for the kill. He smashed at the big pulpy face with terrible blows, beating Thompson to his knees. He made one more effort to get going, but Matt moved away from his grasping hands, slapped a blow aside, and countered with a right to the face.

Circling warily, still wary of the big man's strength, Matt jabbed a left, crossed a right, and moved away, circling slightly. Thompson turned clumsily to face him, and Matt suddenly went in, ducked a swing and, setting himself, smashed five wicked blows to the head and face, followed by a ripping uppercut to the wind. As Thompson started to fall, Matt caught him by the hair and jerking him up, smashed him again in the face before he dropped him.

Deliberately then, he walked over to Felton and took back his gunbelt. At the water trough he splashed water over his face and held his hands under the pipe that emptied cold water into the trough. Then from Clyde he took a shotgun.

"All right," he said. He motioned to Thompson, who lay sprawled and bloody in the dust. "Take him away.

"Peggoty, you and Thompson be out of town before daylight tomorrow, or I'll throw you both in the bottom of the deepest shaft around here and leave you there until it rains."

Gorman nodded dumbly, staring unbelievingly at Big Thompson, whom he had believed invincible.

The crowd still waited, as if expecting something more. "Any of you whose names are on that list," Coburn said, "are advised to leave. Any who don't will be given a chance to shoot it out. I'm cleaning up ... we'll run this town clean, we'll run it honest. Have all the fun you want, but I'll stand for no crooked work."

He turned and walked back up the street to Felton's cabin. Once inside, he put down the shotgun and sagged into a chair, breathing slowly and painfully.

"You hurt?" Cohan asked.

Matt looked around and said wryly, "He could punch, Dan. Every time he hit me, it hurt."

"Will this end it?"

"No." Matt Coburn waited a moment, breathing heavily. "No, this won't end it. I'll need my guns now. And there's still Kingsbury. This won't impress him, not a bit. Nor Ike Fletcher."

Suddenly the door opened, and Tucker Dolan stood there. "Matt, there's a lady to see you."

Matt got to his feet shakily. The reaction had set in now; his muscles were trembling, and he felt sick at his stomach. "All right. I'll see her. Come in, Madge."

Only it wasn't Madge—it was Laurie Shannon.

If Laurie had heard the name she made no comment, but said only, "Matt, are you all right?"

She saw his face then, as he turned toward her. "Oh, Matt! Your poor face!"

He looked in the mirror. There was a dark welt under

his right eye, a cut over the left one, and his jaw was swollen. He touched it tenderly. "I wasn't expecting to see you here," he said. "Laurie, you'd better leave. This has only started."

"We thought you might need help. Tucker wanted to come, and so did Joss." She smiled. "I found that I wanted to come with them, and we're going to stay ... if you don't object."

Abruptly, Matt sat down. "Sorry," he said, "I'm still kind of shaky."

He stared at his hands. The knuckles were cut and swollen. His fingers were bruised and sore, and he worked them cautiously. Desperately he wanted to try them on a gun, but did not dare while anyone could see. He knew all too well how people would talk, even the best-intentioned ones. Moreover, he did not want anyone's fear for him to communicate itself to him. The one thing he had going for him in that lawless crowd was fear ... a fear born of knowledge of his skill with a gun.

He might have been a fool to beat Big Thompson with his fists, but he hoped the roughest element could be demoralized by his doing so. If he could defeat their leader, their bully, he might win without killing anyone else. But two men were dead ... and he felt sure there would be others.

He looked at Clyde. "Have you seen Fletcher?" he asked.

"No sign of him. Nobody's seen him for hours. Or any of his crowd, for that matter."

"I've got to stop them."

Nobody spoke. Matt's head was hanging and he closed his eyes. His head throbbed, and his eyes burned. Just closing them was relief. His knuckles, too, throbbed heavily, but he kept flexing and unflexing his fingers. He dare not let them get stiff, but they were thick and clumsy, and he did not know if he could even hold a gun.

"Dick," he said, "keep an eye on the street for me, will you?"

Tucker spoke up. "Matt, you want me to take a walk down in the town? I might find somebody who'd talk. I know most of that bunch with Fletcher."

"Be careful."

Dolan disappeared through the door, and Laurie went to the stove, stirred up the fire, and put on a kettle.

Matt was aching in every muscle, not only with bruises, but with weariness. His very bones ached. Thompson had been such a big man to fight, and the very effort of hitting him, wrestling with him, and pushing him off had taken Matt's strength. He forced himself to consider what lay ahead.

Slowly his mind considered those whose names he had listed. How many of them would leave?

Simmons came in. "The stage is leaving," he said, "and she's full. We're getting a wagon that will go as far as Ely . . . sixteen men are going in it."

Well, that was a few of them, anyway.

Felton, standing close by, finally spoke. "Coburn, I owe you an apology. I made a damned fool of myself."

"You tried. You're too decent a man, Felton—they don't operate that way. They take decency for weakness, and weakness represents opportunity to them. You're a good man, but you've lived too long in an orderly civilization. It's different out here in the open."

He paused, holding his fingers against his swollen eye. "I'm one of them, you see. I can be a wolf among the wolves."

"Thanks, anyway. You pulled me out of a hole."

Felton went out, and walked up to the collar of the shaft where Zeller was waiting. Zeller threw him a sharp glance. "Somedings iss wrong?"

"His hands. They're in awful shape, Zeller. I don't see how he can draw a gun."

"Broken?"

"No . . . but bruised and swollen. It was one hell of a fight. I wouldn't have believed anybody could whip Thompson with his fists, but Coburn did it, and good, too."

Zeller looked down at the town and said, "Somedimes the goodt dings come hardt, Dick. Idt iss nodt easy to buildt a town."

Back in the house, Laurie brought a pan of water to the table beside Matt. "Sit up now. I'm going to sponge off your face."

Carefully, she began to wipe away the dried blood and to clean around the cuts. She indicated his hands. "What are you going to do about those? You can't go down there tonight."

"I have to."

"They'll be waiting for you, Matt. They'll know your hands are in bad shape."

"I laid down the law. I've got to enforce it."

She sat down beside him. "Matt, why did you do it? You told me you were through with all this."

"The town was in trouble, and they had Felton in a corner."

"Was it the town, or was it Madge Healy"

"The town. Oh, sure, Madge needed help. She still does."

Laurie's lips tightened a little. He grinned at her.

"Don't look like that. She's a girl alone, fighting a tough fight. I helped you with those cow thieves, didn't I?"

"Yes, but—"

He smiled and got up, flexing his hands. Then he suddenly remembered what she had told him. "You said Joss came with you. Where is he?"

"I don't know. He turned off somewhere down the street on some business of his own. He didn't say what it was."

He looked at her. "Dorset's in town. I should have put his name on the list, but I didn't."

"I don't think he's really bad, Matt. I really don't. He's just got a lot of foolish notions."

"He thinks he's a gunman," Matt replied. "I don't know of any faster way to get yourself killed."

The day drew on slowly. The stage left and then two

wagons followed. Several riders could be seen along the trail, but there were too few of them, Matt thought.

Suddenly he sat up. "Tobe Burnside! Laurie—"

Tucker Dolan stood in the doorway. "What about him?" he interrupted. "If you're askin' if he's gone, he ain't. He's in the Bucket waitin' for you."

"What else did you hear?"

"Fletcher and his crowd are holed up back in the canyon waiting for some word from Kingsbury. It seems Kingsbury sent a rider out of town to get somebody, somebody who's job it'll be to get you if you interfere."

Matt looked at Dolan thoughtfully. "Now who would that be? Just who would he send for?"

"You know as well as me. There's only one man around who'd want to brace you with a gun in your hand."

"Who?" Laurie asked. "Who does he mean, Matt?"

"Bell," Matt replied. "Calvin Bell."

CHAPTER 17

Laurie bathed Matt's swollen hands with hot water, hoping to take away some of the stiffness and to get the blood to circulating properly.

Tucker Dolan had left, but he returned again to tell Matt that twenty-seven of the names on the list could be checked off, for five women and twenty-two men had already left town. But the doors of Burnside's Bucket of Blood remained open, and Tobe Burnside was at the bar ... waiting.

"They're ready for you, Matt. It's a trap if I ever saw one. Let me go down there for you. My hands are in good shape, and they won't be expecting anything from me."

"It's my job, Tuck. But thanks, anyway."

Matt lay back on the cot, his head throbbing with a dull, heavy ache. He had taken some wicked punishment, and he could feel it now, but his mind worked on the problem presented by the Bucket.

Mentally he drew a picture of the layout, both inside and on the street. Tobe was a tough man, and he must be gambling on Matt's bad hands and the possibilities for a fist fight.... And there was Ike Fletcher, who had taken this as his opportunity to remove one who was a danger.

Despite the dull ache in his head and the soreness in

156

his body, Matt forced himself to concentrate. To win the struggle that faced him, he must consider every move, plan for every possibility. Tucker Dolan would help, but Matt worked better alone. Then there would be no one to get in the way, no one but himself to consider. He liked it that way; for he had no tendency to lean on anyone, to depend on anyone but himself.

Long ago he had learned that problems could often be solved by that part of the mind that worked beneath the surface; that, given the elements of a problem, it was the nature of the mind to attempt to solve it, or at least to cope with it. The first essential was to see clearly what the problem was, to frame the problem correctly, and the means of solving it would often come without too much working at it.

He had turned his reactions in the same way. The body of every man, like the body of every animal, contains those factors necessary for survival, and one could not depend only on what was consciously seen and heard. One must depend on the subtle senses beyond the range of consciousness, the movements beyond the periphery of one's vision, and even on changes of atmosphere, on the actual feeling of menace.

But always the first thing was to state the problem to one's self, to alert the senses by this means. The senses, if made use of, had a way of developing, growing even more sensitive. And over the years Matt Coburn had come, like many another such man, to depend upon the subconscious feelings.

In considering his problem now he was not only consciously considering what might be done to trap him and what moves he could make to avoid the trap, but he was preparing himself mentally for what was to come, he was conditioning his body and his mind, and these would control his muscles and his reactions.

Finally, he sat up and dried his hands. Did they actually feel better, or was he imagining it?

Tucker started to speak again. "Matt—"

"Don't say it, Tuck. You don't like that bunch down

there any more than I do, but I took on the job, and it's me they are waiting for."

Laurie had gone to the window and was looking down the street. "It's awfully quiet," she said.

Suddenly there were footsteps outside, and then the door opened and Madge stepped in. "Matt—" She broke off on seeing Laurie. "Oh, I'm sorry."

"It's quite all right," Laurie said. "I'm just a friend."

Madge looked at her and smiled. "If you are, you're crazy," she said. "He's a mighty good man going to waste."

She turned back to Matt. "If you're going down there tonight, go loaded for bear. Big Thompson and Peg Gorman sneaked back into town, and they're hiding out at the Bucket. That's what I came to tell you."

"Thanks, Madge."

That might explain it. If they were hiding at the Bucket, it would be enough to give Burnside confidence. Matt did not like it.

Suddenly he made up his mind. "I'm going to let him sweat," he said aloud. "Tobe is waiting for me to come down there. He's all geared and ready, and there's nothing harder than waiting to spring a trap. The longer you wait, the less ready you are."

He loaded his pockets with shotgun shells and, taking the gun, he went out, carrying it in his left hand, and strolled down the street to the Main Chance. As he went in the front door, somebody ran out the back, but Matt made no attempt to follow. For a few minutes he watched a poker game, then he went across the street to the Nugget, and after that to the Sixty. In none of the places did he see any of those he had ordered out of town.

He walked on down the street and talked briefly to Buckwalter, then turned back abruptly. He thought of the tension in Burnside's Bucket of Blood, where they would be wondering and waiting. He went into the Bon-Ton and ordered a cup of coffee and sat where he could watch the street.

He took his time over the coffee, and after a few

minutes he saw a man emerge from the Bucket and stand idly on the walk. It was Kid Curtis.

After a few minutes Curtis went back inside, and Matt smiled grimly. He was prepared to wait, and in comfort.

From his position at the window of the Bon-Ton he had a clear view of the street. The coffee tasted good, and suddenly he was feeling better. He decided he was feeling better because he was doing something at which he was good.

It was like a chess game, he supposed—although he had never played chess—with the difference that he had several opponents, and while moving against one he must never forget the others who might choose that moment to move against him. And of course, he thought grimly, the stakes were higher in this game. A wrong move meant death.

He preferred to move quickly, to get his enemies off balance and never let them get set. He preferred to drive hard and straight ahead, but in this case he would wait, and he was like an Indian for patience. They would grow more tense as time went on, more uncomfortable, more irritable, and more apt to move too quickly and rashly when they did move.

Thompson, Gorman, and Curtis ... three dangerous men. Tobe Burnside, too, although Matt had an idea that Tobe would not move until his move could be decisive. Since Curtis was there, Skin Weber might also be, although Skin might be inclined to act on his own.

Fletcher and Kingsbury would not be involved in this, but they probably knew of it. This was not their kind of play. Matt ordered another cup of coffee and sat back.

Would they finally move against him? When he did not appear, would they leave their trap and try to hunt him down? This was the point to be considered.

Now a man appeared in front of the Bucket, and strolled idly up the street ... too idly altogether. It was Alec, an occasional shill at gambling games, and sometimes a swamper in the saloons. Matt was quite sure that

Alec was being sent up the street to find out just what he was doing.

A shabby, down-at-the-heels man, Alec walked along, pausing now and again to peer into doorways. When he reached the Bon-Ton he was about to pass by when he glanced in the window and saw Matt sitting there. He stopped abruptly, started as if to go on, then turned and came into the restaurant.

The Bon-Ton was empty except for Matt, and as Alec entered, Matt ordered another cup of coffee. "Bring me a pot of it," he added. "I haven't felt so relaxed in a long time."

Alec sat down at another table, ordered coffee and a piece of pie. He looked at Matt from time to time with quick, curious glances.

As Matt filled his cup, Laurie came through the door. He indicated the pot. "Sit down and have some coffee. This is the first time I've had a chance to rest and relax since I hit town."

Laurie glanced at Alec and sat down. "Look," Matt said in a lower tone, but one still audible to Alec, "I can move against those boys down the street any time. Let 'em worry. Are the boys up the street armed and ready?"

Laurie realized at once that Matt was speaking for effect, although she had no idea who Alec was, or why he might be important.

"Yes," she said, "they're ready."

"Good! Now let's talk about you." Matt slipped easily into conversation about the ranch and about Laurie's plans, bringing out casually the fact that Tucker Dolan was in town.

"When he knew you were in for a fight," Laurie said, "he couldn't stay away, Matt. Joss is in town too."

Alec finished his coffee, paid for it, and slipped out the door.

Instantly Matt was on his feet. "Stay here and keep out of the way," he said to Laurie. "I'm going down there."

He went quickly through to the rear door, and looked both ways. The Bon-Ton's back door could not be seen from anywhere but the surrounding hills, and Matt saw that they were empty. He went outside and moved down the backs of the buildings, ducking below windows, using what cover he could. He was at the rear door of the Bucket of Blood when Alec walked in the front door.

He heard Alec say, "He's just a-settin' up there, drinkin' coffee an' lallygaggin' with that Shannon woman from the Rafter—seems to have all the time in the world. But he's cookin' somethin'."

"What d'you mean?" Burnside asked.

"Some of that crowd up at Discovery are all armed and waitin'. Tucker Dolan's there, too—you know, that Arizona gunfighter. An' they mentioned somebody called Joss."

"Joss Ringgold," Gorman said. "He's an old outlaw who's been workin' for that Shannon girl. He's a real ol' curly wolf, that one."

"What d'you suppose he's got in mind?" Curtis asked.

Matt had seen the boot-prints where men had waited outside the back window. The sash was raised, and two men with guns could sweep the floor between the wall and the bar, while they themselves remained under cover. Undoubtedly other men had been concealed elsewhere.

He knew there was no question of getting them to surrender—they simply weren't the type. They had forted up for a fight, and there was no choice—it was fight or die. Matt knew there was no alternative for him.

As Curtis spoke, and before anyone could reply, Matt stepped in, eased the door shut behind him and answered. "Just this, gentlemen. You called the tune, let's see how you dance."

All the men were armed, and three of them had weapons in their hands. As Matt finished speaking, he was firing.

He shot Peggoty Gorman first, because he thought he

might fall against Thompson, disturbing the big man's aim. He shot Gorman right in the belly with the shotgun, then let Curtis have the other barrel. Dropping the shotgun, he went to one knee, to offer a smaller target, drawing as he dropped.

His hand was stiff, but he grasped the six-shooter, brought it level as Thompson's first shot missed by a hair. Matt fired twice, taking his time and pointing his shots low for Thompson's broad hips and belly.

Alec had hit the floor, crying out that he was not armed, which Matt was willing to believe. Flipping a quick shot at Burnside, a shot that missed, Matt dropped the six-gun into its holster and broke the shotgun and removed the empty shells. He had rehearsed this many times and it worked swiftly and smoothly, his slightly stiff fingers bothering him scarcely at all.

As he worked his mind was clicking. He knew what his chances were, and up to a point they were good. The breaks had come his way. Alec had just told them he was up the street talking to a pretty girl, so he had taken them off guard, and their reaction time was in his favor. There would be an instant to register his voice, an instant to turn and face him, to get the reality of his presence. In all, it was only a few seconds, but his first shotgun charge was ripping into Peg Gorman's belly even as he spoke.

Curtis, who got the second barrel, was fast. Kid Curtis had sand, and he had speed. The shotgun blast hit him just as his own gun blasted, but Matt was a split second faster, enough to deflect Curtis' aim.

Curtis was on one knee, fumbling with his left hand for his fallen pistol. Thompson had caught himself after the brief sting of the few shot he must have caught, and he had drawn unbelievably fast. But so had Matt, and Matt had the priceless advantage of knowing every move he was going to make before he made even the first one.

He shot into Thompson, saw the bullet strike, and fired again. Thompson was not falling—he was bracing himself for a shot. He fired ... fired again. Thompson had missed his first shot because of the sting of the grazing slugs and Gorman's fall. His second shot missed as Matt went to his knees.

Thompson brought his gun up again, rested it on his forearm, and fired just as Matt snapped his shotgun into place. As he did so, he threw himself from his half-kneeling position to a resting place on the floor, coming down on his right forearm. His left hand guided the shotgun into position on Thompson's belly, and the right triggered the shot.

A thundering blast, and Thompson raised up on his toes and fell. The jar of Matt's forearm striking the floor had deflected Matt's aim, and the shot, instead of catching Thompson in the stomach, caught him in the throat. He fell, and Matt sprang clear, staggering to his feet.

Thompson and Gorman were dead; Alec was scrambling for the door; Curtis had fallen, but was still struggling to get his left hand around to where his gun lay. Matt stepped over and kicked the gun away, his shotgun bearing on Curtis' face.

For an instant they stared at each other. The slightest squeeze of the trigger and Curtis would be dead, and he knew it. He looked up at Matt, no surrender in him, ready to take the blast if it came. "Go ahead, Coburn," he said. "You earned it. Kill me."

"No." Matt pointed his toe at Curtis' shattered right hand and wrist. "You're through as a gunman, Kid. You get out of here, change your name, and act as if you never heard of a gun."

Only then did he really look over at Tobe Burnside, though a corner of his eye had never missed a move the saloonkeeper made.

Tobe had both hands on the bar in plain sight. His face was a study in shock, but he was trying to show that he wasn't fighting, that he was out of it.

Matt Coburn walked away from Curtis and looked

across the bar at Tobe. The big man's lips were trembling, his face was ashen.

"I gave you a chance to leave, Tobe," Matt said, almost conversationally. "You didn't take it."

"I was a damn fool."

"Yes, you were," Matt said, and he smashed the butt of the shotgun into Tobe's teeth.

Burnside staggered back and Matt vaulted the bar, shoving him from behind it toward the door. "There's the road," he said. "Get off down the trail before I change my mind."

"Wait, I gotta get—"

"You get nothing. Yesterday you could have taken what you wanted. Now you get nothing but a running start."

Tobe burst through the door and went down in the street sprawling. He got up, staggered, and started down the trail. Buckwalter walked up beside Matt, who stood outside the door. "You lettin' him go like that"

"Yeh. On the Barbary Coast he robbed and helped to shanghai hundreds of men, poor sailors ashore from their ships, or country boys who didn't know what a place they'd gotten into. He got out of 'Frisco just ahead of a lynching party, but he never learned a thing. Maybe he'll learn from this, though I doubt it."

Matt went back inside and locked the back door, then he went out the front, shut the door behind him, and locked it.

As he turned he saw Alec trying to get back into the crowd that had gathered, and he motioned to him. Hesitantly, the swamper came up to him. "Alec," Matt said, "you traveled with the wrong crowd. You might have been killed in there."

"I guess so. I thought of that."

"Take this." Matt handed him the key. "Go in there and take those two men out to Boot Hill and bury them deep. Put markers over them—any man deserves that— and you can take whatever money is in the till. Then you light out of here."

Alec hesitated. "I take the money?"

"Take it. Most of it is stolen money. Use it to buy yourself an outfit and make a start—but first you bury those men, do you hear?"

Matt was tired. He stood on the street and watched the crowd slowly disperse. He reloaded his shotgun, then his pistol. Tired as he was, his hands aching, his swollen eye throbbing, he was alert and watching, for he was not through yet. Skin Weber was around, and there were others . . . dozens of them.

He walked back up the street, every step an effort. At the Bon-Ton he went in. Laurie was still there, and she came quickly to him. He slumped into a chair.

"Coffee," he said. "Make it hot and strong."

She poured the coffee, sadness in her eyes. "How many, Matt?"

"Two . . . Thompson and Gorman."

"That's four, Matt. Four men, right in this town."

"I didn't keep count."

"But *four* men, Matt!"

"Don't look at me like that, Laurie. And if you want to count, count up the number of men murdered and robbed by those four. . . .

"That committee up there . . . the ones who want to build a fine town, with schools and all. They didn't hire me for my beauty. They hired me because they thought I could do a job none of them could do. And when it's over? They'll get shut of me as fast as they can. I know that, and still I do it. I'm a fool, Laurie, and maybe it's just as well that you've decided you despise me."

"But I don't—"

"If you don't," he said, "you will. Everybody wants the job done, but they don't have to like the man who does it."

He got up, staggering a little from sheer exhaustion, and he walked out of the door and up the street. He would sleep in some out-of-the-way place tonight, without a fire. He'd have to find a place where he could just cave in, where he could lie down and let go, with no fear in him.

And where would that be? Where . . . this side of the grave?

CHAPTER 18

He was a man alone. He took his rifle and walked out on the bare hillside and sat down in full view of the town.

The slope went up behind him to the distant crest. He would be no easy rifle shot from up there, and there was no way a man could get there without his knowing, unless the man made a long roundabout swing that would take hours. They could see him from the town, but he could see them, too, so he sat up there and stared down at Confusion.

Laurie was lost to him . . . but when had she been his? When had it been more than an idea in his mind, and one to which he had not dared give hope?

He could ride out now; but he had never backed off from a job or left one half-finished. And there was Madge to think of, fighting a lone fight against a combination too tough for any girl to tackle.

She had Pike, of course. A good man with a gun, but how smart was he? How good would he be when Kingsbury started plotting?

Matt Coburn stared at his swollen hands and swore, slowly, bitterly. He should not have taken the job. He had known what it meant, what he would have to do. What was there in him that would not allow him to walk away from such a job?

Did he like to kill?

Slowly, his head throbbing dully, he considered that. In all honesty ... did he?

No.

He could have killed Curtis and Burnside. Curtis was a good kid heading down a wrong trail, so there was a reason to let him go; but Burnside? He was a murderer and a thief, a man who had helped to shanghai many a poor soul, and had robbed them first. No telling how many men he had put through that trap door over the bay in his place on Barbary Coast. Or later, in other places, for that matter. Why hadn't he killed Tobe Burnside?

No, he did not like to kill, but he could not recall that he felt much remorse, either, over those who had died by his gun. If it had been Curtis, or a kid like Dorset— yes. But not the others. They were mature men, hard men, men who came at him armed and ready, and they took their chances, as he took his.

Even Big Thompson. The man was a brute without any redeeming qualities, except that of courage. When the chips were down he had stood up there and tried— you had to give him that. And he was still trying when he went out.

Whipping Thompson had taken a lot out of Matt, and the tension ... waiting for the moment to come, and the action that followed ... it left a man wrung out like an old rag.

One more day. One more day should do it, and then he was going over there where the tall mountain was, the one with the glacier. He was going up to one of those high green parks among the aspen, and he was going to stay there for a week ... maybe for two or three. He would stay there alone, just sleeping, eating, and thinking of nothing at all.

And then he was going to take the unknown trails out of this country, and he was going to ride and ride until he reached a place where nobody had ever heard of Matt Coburn.

The trouble was, a man could not escape from himself, and wherever he would go, in the kind of country in which he could make a living, there would always be a need for a Matt Coburn.

There were a lot of good folks in the world, but there were a lot of others who underneath the veneer were savages, savages, just waiting for a chance to do what they wanted to do if they could do it without fear of punishment. And nature and the years of living had given Matt Coburn the kind of stuff it took to walk the dark streets and bring restraint to those who hated restraint.

Slowly his muscles relaxed. He worked himself into an easier position, still staring down at the town. A stage was leaving, and by the look of it, it was carrying a heavy load. Some of the others on his list were on it, he knew, some who had now become believers. They would ride on to another town and begin all over again. One or two might decide it was not worth the risk, and would seek easier, safer occupations.

Up here it was cold now, and he felt a chill in his muscles, but he did not want to move. Besides, he had no place to go. He would wait here until dark, then he would go down into the town again. He would pass the word around to the last few, and he would see what could be done about Kingsbury and Fletcher.

Those two were not going to be easy. Kingsbury was no gunman, even though he hired gunmen—he was a man who used money, power, and good lawyers, but always there was somebody like Ike Fletcher standing between him and whatever was to be done that might be illegal. You could not kill a man without hanging for it, and it was a sure thing that Kingsbury would never be caught packing a gun for that purpose.

As Matt waited he dozed, and the shadows crept along the hill. Those down below could not tell that he was dozing, and they watched him, sitting all alone on the barren hill, a dark figure waiting there above the town like a crouching beast.

"What's he thinking about, do you suppose?" Felton asked uneasily. "Why is he up there alone?"

"Four men are dead," Simmons said, "... just like that. And Curtis is crippled."

"He's been doin' the job you hired him for," Fife said testily. "The job none of us could do."

"Yes, but four men have been killed." Jim Gage shook his head doubtfully. "He could have arrested them ... or something. And Burnside ... he wouldn't even let him close out his business—just drove him off."

"It seems to me, Jim," Fife said, "that you were about to pull out. You'd given up on the town."

"Well ... I changed my mind. A man can change his mind, can't he? And with Thompson gone ..."

"It'll be different, won't it?" Fife said. "You'll feel safer now. You'll feel safer because Matt Coburn killed him, and ran off the rest of them."

"I don't hold with killing," Gage protested. "Four men ... that's too much."

"You find some other way to do it, Jim. You just do that, and I'll run your story in the biggest type I've got."

When it was dark Matt Coburn came down into the town again and walked along the street. He stopped in here and there, and passed on. Nobody spoke to him, nobody seemed to notice him. On one dark street he saw a girl standing in a doorway smoking a cigarette. He could see the sheen of light on her silk dress.

"Hello, Mattie," he said.

"How are you, Matt?"

"That man of yours around?"

"You've run him off, Matt. He pulled out."

"I'm sorry, Mattie, but you know what he's like."

"I know."

"Why don't you give him up, Mattie? He'll get you in big trouble some day."

"I know he will." The cigarette glowed, and she went on, "I love him, Matt. Does that make sense to you?"

He was silent a moment, this lonely man with a heavy

gun on his hip. "You bet it does, Mattie. You hang onto him then, but try to keep him straight, will you?"

"I'll try, Matt. I do try." She paused. "I ain't much myself, you know. I'm not able to talk much without him telling me what I am."

"You're a good woman, Mattie. I've known you in four towns now—"

"Five, Matt. You forgot Leadville."

"All right ... five. Five towns, Mattie, and you've always been square. And when the boys had cholera down in Bensonville, you stayed on. When everybody else left, you stayed."

"What else could I do?"

He shifted the rifle to his other hand. "So long, Mattie. See you around."

"S'long Matt."

He went back to the main street and stood there in the darkness, watching the town. It was quiet tonight. The saloons and gambling places were almost empty. Business would pick up tomorrow ... but he would be gone then. Tucker ... Tucker Dolan would be the man for them then.

There was just one more job for him to do. He had to stop Ike Fletcher and Kingsbury.

Suddenly there was a rush of horses and a loud yell from up the street. A buckboard wheeled around the corner so wildly that it careened against the corner of a building and turned over, spilling its one occupant into the street.

One? No ... there were two. A man fell from the back of the buckboard, and as he rolled the light shone on his face. It was Pike Sides.

The other ... it was Madge Healy, struggling to her feet. "Matt! Oh, my God! Matt, help me!"

Then they came around the corner in a rush, Ike Fletcher in the lead. He was whirling a rope, and as Pike Sides started to rise, the rope dropped around him and jerked him down. Before Fletcher could start to drag him, Matt sprang into the street.

"Ike! Stop it!"

"You go to hell!" Fletcher roared, and several riders whipped around past him, ropes whirling.

Matt made a wild dive for the side of the building and turned, firing his Winchester. A rider spilled into the street, and Matt saw Pike stagger to his feet, saw an empty holster.

"Pike!" he called. The gunman turned, and Matt tossed him his spare pistol.

Pike Sides took it out of the air, and emptied a saddle with his first shot. Fletcher spurred his horse, and Matt fired as Pike did, and Fletcher reeled in the saddle.

Suddenly armed men were closing in all around Matt, and he heard the hammer of guns. Something slugged him and he felt a wave of sickness go over him. But he was firing, firing, and then he clubbed the Winchester and waded in.

A rope ripped the Winchester from his hands, and a racing rider struck him viciously across the face with a coiled rope. Blinded, Matt grabbed for his six-shooter as another rope dropped around him. A horse rushed past him and he was jerked hard, and with a wild yell the rider started to drag him.

From the side of a building a gun blasted, and the rider above him went out of the saddle. Matt rolled over, fighting clear of the coil of rope.

Then he saw the one who had fired the shot. It was Mattie!

And then a door burst open and Nathan Bly was on the walk, gun in hand. Standing like a duelist, he was firing, and at every shot a saddle emptied.

Matt shook off the rope and climbed to his feet. Something slugged him again and he went down firing. He came part way up, and Kendrick loomed before him, a shotgun aimed at Matt's face. Matt fired, and saw Kendrick's face wiped out in a mask of blood. The shotgun went off with a roar, and the charge hit the earth beside Matt, spewing dirt and sand into his face.

Matt lunged to his feet, staggering. He saw Dorset

staring at him, white-faced and wide-eyed. "Get out of here," Matt roared, "or I'll kill you!"

Amazingly, Dorset ducked and ran.

The Fletcher riders had turned at the bottom of the street and were coming back. Matt had fallen again, but he staggered up. There was blood in his eyes, blood soaking his shirt. Swaying, he stood there waiting the charge, but something made him turn.

Mattie was beside him, then Madge, holding a pistol. Close by was Joss Ringgold, his face set hard as he waited for the riders; then Nathan Bly and Sturd Fife, and now Felton and Zeller were coming.

The riders started with a rush, and the small group waiting in the street held their fire as if on command; then they all fired as one person, and after that at will. The column of riders melted before them. A horse ran off, dragging a screaming rider.

Matt went down again, and as he fell he caught a glimpse of a white face in a window across the street, the face of a man watching. It was Kingsbury.

Matt rolled over and came up with his gun, but there was no strength in him. But a sudden shot came from above him, and he saw that it was Nathan Bly, and he was pointing across the street.

Matt tried to get up, and then everything seemed drowned in a thunder of sound that ended with the pop, pop, of guns, seemingly from far away.

It seemed only a moment later that he opened his eyes. He was lying on the floor of the Bon-Ton, and from where he lay he could see Nathan Bly standing in the doorway with a rifle, and Tucker Dolan and Joss Ringgold were at windows. Matt looked up to see that his head was in Madge Healy's lap. Mattie was cutting away his shirt. Sturd Fife, Zeller, Dan Cohan, and Felton were all in the room.

"How is it?" Matt asked. "What's happened?"

"It's quiet," Fife said. "Seem to me she's over. Somebody shot Kingsbury, killed him dead ... stray bullet, more'n likely."

Matt looked down at himself. Mattie was washing the blood away, and he could see a hole where a bullet had gone in.

"How bad am I?"

"You caught four slugs, Matt, and you've lost a lot of blood."

He closed his eyes, feeling no pain, just weakness and the stiffness in his sore hands and face. Mattie was as good as most doctors, he knew that, and she'd had a lot of experience with gunshot wounds.

There was no sound in the room but the occasional creak of a board as somebody shifted his weight, or moved about. And for a long time there was no sound from the street outside. He could feel Mattie probing for a bullet now, and it was no longer just the stiffness that he felt. Suddenly he heard a call from the street. The voice was unfamiliar.

"You in there! We want to pick up Fletcher. Is it all right?"

"You can pick him up if you want to ride right out of town," Fife bellowed. "We want none of you here."

"Who's that talkin'? Ain't Matt Coburn in there?"

"Matt's out scoutin' for you boys," Dolan said, speaking loud enough for them to hear. "My guess is he'll pick up a couple of scalps before mornin'."

There was a sound of whispers, then the speaker said. "Hell, we're not fightin' no more. We're fresh out of work. Somebody shot Kingsbury."

"He's had it comin'," Fife said, "and I'll print that."

"We're pullin' out," the speaker said. "You call off Coburn, d'you hear?"

They rode away down the street, and there was silence again. After a while a cock crowed somewhere down the valley, and Madge spoke quietly. "If one of you boys will round up a buckboard we can take Matt to my ranch."

Suddenly Matt gasped and Mattie exclaimed: "I got it! I got the slug!"

"We'd best keep him in town, ma'am," Felton said. "There's too many around still who don't like him."

It was morning when Matt opened his eyes again. Somebody had brought a bed into the Bon-Ton and he was lying near the window.

Madge Healy was asleep in a chair nearby, and Joss Ringgold sat in the doorway with a shotgun across his knees.

Matt raised his head, and the effort turned him giddy. He let his head fall back, but Joss had seen his movement. He tiptoed over. "Don't want to wake her," he whispered. "She's stayed right by you all night."

"What's happening?"

"It's quiet. Some of the mines have gone back to work. Jim Gage has his store open. I think most of the rough crowd are gone." Joss dropped to his heels. "I think you done it, Matt. I think you cleaned her up."

"What happened?" He indicated Madge. "To her, I mean?"

"Fletcher used ropes. He snared the guards up there, dragged one of them to death, another almost. Madge, she broke loose and came down here in her buckboard and smashed it up, like you know.

"They roped Pike. Last thing he was lookin' for, an' it was just the way Fletch planned it. They dragged him down here. He broke loose, swung into the back of the buckboard just before she crashed. Then you threw down on them.

"Fletch was killed, Kendrick is dead, and Smoke is dead. Scarff is badly shot up, but he may pull through. A few more of those boys caught some lead, but they pulled out fast after Kingsbury was killed. Those boys fight for money, and when he went down and they found out about it, why, they just scattered."

Matt closed his eyes. Outside, he could hear people passing along the street, and the sound of people working. It was all over, then ... it was finished. He lay still, having no desire to move or to talk, only to rest, in that strange lethargy that had come over him.

But he opened his eyes. "What about the restaurant?" he asked. "I've got to get out of here, Joss."

Even as he said it, he knew he did not want to move, and he closed his eyes again. At this moment he felt as if he never wanted to move again.

Yet after a few minutes he opened his eyes and looked out into the sunlit street. It wasn't much of a street, and it wasn't much of a town. Fifty years from now there probably would be nothing here ... maybe a foundation or two, some holes in the hillside, and markers up there on the graves of the men who had died.

Felton would have his church and his school, and for a few years the town would have a life, and then it would fade, and the coyotes would howl on Boot Hill, the buzzards would swing idly above, and maybe a chipmunk would dig where the miners had been and gone.

"Joss, it isn't much of a town, is it?" he said.

"They never are, not when they're startin'. But this one's a better place today than it was yesterday."

Matt turned to look at him. "You got away from the wild life, Joss. Do you ever get the feeling you'd like to go back to it?"

"Who doesn't, sometimes? The wild night rides, the sudden raids—oh, it was excitin' and all, but mostly it was hidin' out in some place unfit for man or beast, goin' without proper food or drink, never goin' to sleep without expectin' to jump up and run for it if a posse came. No, Matt, I'm a comfort-lovin' man today."

"Are you going back to the ranch?"

Joss stirred uneasily. "I ain't sure. Miss Shannon, she came over here to help—we all did. But somehow ... well, she don't hold with killin' and it sort of got to her. Folks like that, they just figure there's got to be something wrong with you if you've killed that many men. They never seem to figure that those men were tryin' to kill you, an' you just happened to be faster or luckier, or something. Anyway, she got upset and went back to the ranch."

When Matt woke again, it was already night, and lights had begun to appear in the buildings along the street. Madge was beside his bed.

"I'm worried about the Bon-Ton," Matt said. "They're losing business."

"Don't worry about it," Madge said. "I bought it. All you have to do is get well."

"What about the town? They'll need some law."

"They've got it. I told them what you said about Dolan. Oh, I know! You didn't really tell me, but you muttered about it, and I told them and they've hired him."

"Where's Joss?"

"He rode out to the ranch to pick up his gear. He will be back tonight."

"Pike?"

"He's coming along. He'd been wounded before we left the mine, and then they dragged him. He's in bad shape, but he'll pull through."

For a while they sat silent. Matt felt better, although he was weak. "Where's my gun?" he asked suddenly.

"Hanging right beside you." Madge pointed to the gunbelt and holster hanging on the bedpost. "Tucker put it there. And incidentally, Pike sent you back your spare ... with thanks. You've no idea how impressed he was at your tossing him that gun. He's a strange man, Matt, and I doubt if anybody ever helped him out in his life before. He's mentioned that gun five or six times. Can't seem to get it out of his head."

Matt shrugged. "He needed it, I had it. It was as simple as that."

She went to the table and picked up the gun and brought it to him. "It's loaded, Matt. Pike said you'd want it that way."

Madge turned away. "I'll make coffee, Matt. You just rest a little and try to sleep."

Matt took the spare gun and pushed it down under the covers beside his leg. He had lived too long with a gun not to feel helpless without one. He closed his eyes and rested.

He could hear vague sounds from the kitchen, and occasionally somebody passed along the boardwalk. It was very quiet here, and he dozed. Only a few minutes could have passed, he supposed, for Madge Healy was still in the kitchen.

She would be coming back soon. He heard a soft, ever so soft footstep. Vaguely he felt a strange disquiet, a restlessness, but not enough to bring him awake. That step sounded again, very gently.

Out on the street somebody was running. He heard a heavy fall, a cry, and then a scrambling of feet.

Then came a cry: "Matt! Matt! *Look out!*"

Suddenly Matt was wide awake, his fist closed on the gun butt. Had he been dreaming?

He heard another, more feeble cry: "Matt! It's Cal . . ."

The voice faded, and Matt lay wide-eyed in the dark room. A board creaked, and Matt turned slightly to his right side to face the door in the back wall. One door led to the kitchen, and the other, in the back wall, opened into a hallway that led to two rooms of living quarters and to a back door.

Matt passed the pistol from his left side over to his right, taking it in his right hand and easing back the blankets a little.

Where was Madge? He found himself praying that something would keep her in the kitchen.

But who had warned him? Who could have called out, and what had happened out there?

He waited, his mouth dry. He felt as weak as a cat. Turning on his side had been an effort.

A figure loomed in the doorway, the dark figure of a man holding a gun.

"Hello, Matt." There was confidence in the tone, confidence and triumph.

"Hello, Cal," Matt said. "I wasn't really expecting you, now that Kingsbury's dead."

"He paid me in advance, Matt. You know that's the only way I'll work. And besides, this is one I would have done just for the pleasure of it. I never liked you, Matt."

"No reason why you should ... or shouldn't. Unless you figured I was better than you. If you believed that, I can see why you might not like me."

Calvin Bell laughed, but there was no humor in the sound. "You? Better than me? We'll never know, will we, Matt? Because I'm going to kill you.

"In a way," Bell went on, "I like it this way. Kind of galls you, doesn't it? Lyin' there helpless, and not a thing you can do."

Outside there was a dragging sound on the boardwalk, and what might have been a groan of both helplessness and anger.

"You always were a talking man, Cal, and you jump to conclusions. I wouldn't fool you, Cal. I've got a gun."

Bell chuckled. "Still bluffin'. I got to hand it to you."

"Well, suppose you loan me your spare, Cal? You always carry insurance on you, so loan it to me and we'll shoot it out even ... or are you scared?"

Somebody was at the front door now, somebody who was trying to get up, to reach the door knob. Calvin heard it, too, and he lifted his gun.

At that moment Madge stepped into the room. "Matt, don't touch this coffee until I get a light. I'll—"

Calvin Bell swung his gun toward her, then realizing it was a woman, he started to swing it back. And Matt shot him.

He thought the shot missed, and lunging up as Bell fired, he heard the bullet smack into the bed where he had been, and then he fired again. Bell half turned toward him, and Matt held the gun steady with both hands. Bell lunged at him, striking the gun aside and jamming the muzzle of his own gun against Matt's belly.

At that instant, Madge spoke. "Mr. Bell? If you'd like to sit down, you may join us for coffee."

The sheer incongruity of it stopped him. Calvin Bell, about to kill a man, heard that cool, quiet voice suggesting that he join them for coffee. For a moment his mind was blank, struggling to adjust itself, and in that instant Matt Coburn came to his feet and shoved Bell away from him.

As he did so, both men fired. Bell was falling away, and his shot missed. Matt, braced on his feet, held the gun steady and shot into Bell as fast as he could work the hammer under his thumb. He knew he would never get another chance, for in a moment he himself was going to fall. He could feel his knees trembling with weakness, and he fired so fast that it sounded like one continuous roll of sound. Then the hammer fell on an empty shell, and the thunder was gone from the room, leaving only the acrid smell of gunpowder. Madge Healy was on her knees, crying.

He swayed as he heard shouts outside, and running feet. They were at the door, and then the door burst open. Matt sat down abruptly, but with the gunfighter's instinct he began thumbing the loading gate open and pushing the empty shells out onto the floor.

Madge caught his arm. "Matt, are you hurt?"

"What happened?" It was Fife's testy voice. "What's going on here, anyway?"

"Strike a light." That was Felton.

Matt fumbled for his cartridge belt. He was scarcely conscious of anything; he only knew that he wanted a loaded gun in his hand.

"It's Calvin Bell," somebody said, "shot to doll rags."

"What's Pike doing outside there?"

Matt looked up. "He tried to warn me—he did warn me. I was asleep, but I heard him. He was yelling, and it jarred me awake, so I was ready when Bell came in."

"Pike's in bad shape. He fell more than once, and dragged himself. . . . I guess he saw Bell coming and knew what he intended to do."

"Are you all right, Matt?" That was Madge again.

"I could do with some coffee." He rolled his legs back

onto the bed and stretched out slowly, painfully. "This place isn't exactly restful."

"Matt, I've got a ranch in Colorado," Madge was saying. "When you're well we'll go there—if you'll make an honest woman of me."

"I'd like that," he said, and eased his tired body on the bed. He was breathing heavily, and one of his wounds felt as if it were bleeding again.

For a week then, he slept, wakened, drank a little soup, slept again. People came and went, but he was scarcely conscious of them. When at last he felt like sitting up, he moved outside into the sunlight.

The town was busy, and it was growing. There was a new general store, a new café, and a hotel was going up. Several of the claims had failed to prove out, but Discovery and the Treasure Vault were showing good values per ton. The Treasure Vault was working forty men in three shifts, the Discovery about the same.

Dick Felton and Dan Cohan stopped by to talk with him. "How're you feeling, Matt?" Cohan asked.

"Better." He looked up at Felton. "I hear you're going to have your school."

"We start building tomorrow."

They talked a while, and then the two men walked away up the street. Matt was feeling restless. When Madge came out, he looked up at her. "Are you tied to this place?" he asked.

"No, Matt. I'm ready when you are." She stood beside him, looking up the street. "You did it, Matt. Confusion has settled down. It's going to be all right."

He nodded. "But they'd like me to leave," he said. "I can see it in their faces. I'm what they don't want around now, Madge. I stand for what they want to forget."

"Shall we start tomorrow, Matt? Shall I bring a rig around?"

"I think so. And Madge, hire Joss, will you? I like him."

"So do I. He'll be driving us, Matt."

He stayed there dozing in the sun, and presently he heard the light quick steps coming, and the swish of skirts. The steps stopped beside him, and he opened his eyes. It was Laurie Shannon.

"You're looking better, Matt."

"I *am* better. We're leaving tomorrow."

Her face seemed to stiffen a little, and there was loneliness in it, and sadness. "Is it Madge, Matt?"

"Yes. We're two of a kind, Laurie. We've both been drifters; we've both seen this country grow."

"Matt, I—"

"Don't say it, Laurie. I killed another man . . . seven it was, I think. You could never live with that."

"No."

"Tomorrow they're starting to build a school, Laurie. The town's going to grow. Sitting here, I see women and youngsters walking by along a street where they never dared walk before. And the town might have gone up in flames."

"And it might not. And seven men are gone who can't be brought back."

"You could have them, Laurie, if you could bring them back. But I think they're better off on Boot Hill."

"I think the town would have lasted. I think those men needn't have died."

"Well—" he shifted his seat—"we'll never know, will we?"

She left him then and walked up the street, and he listened to her footsteps as she walked out of his life. One thing he could give her, though. She sure could make good doughnuts.

He settled back in his chair, enjoying the sun. He'd better rest. It was a long way to Durango.

AUTHOR'S NOTE

Slanting Annie, so called because one leg was shorter than the other, Rocking-Chair Emma, and Mattie were all widely known "madames" in the mining-camp towns and cow towns of the West.

The large lady referred to in the story who assures Matt Coburn that she can handle her own trouble was actually Madame Bulldog, a huge and muscular woman who weighed over 200 pounds, and very little of it fat. She once whipped Martha Jane Canary, better known as Calamity Jane, in a free-for-all fight. She commented afterward that it was no harder than whipping two husky men.

The peak referred to as "Jeff Davis" has since been named Mt. Wheeler and rises above the Snake Range to a height of over 13,000 feet. The peak and the neighboring ranges are heavily forested. There is a glacier on the peak, and a lovely mountain lake high up on a shoulder of the mountain.

The Confusion Mountains are crossed by Highways 50-6 east of Ely, Nevada, and west of Delta, Utah. This is still a wide-open, lonely country where the highway is patrolled by aircraft. The reason for this patrol is simple: if you break down out there, without water on a hot summer's day, you will last no longer than a pioneer in a covered wagon.

ABOUT THE AUTHOR

Louis L'Amour, born Louis Dearborn L'Amour, is of French-Irish descent. Although Mr. L'Amour claims his writing began as a "spur-of-the-moment thing," prompted by friends who relished his verbal tales of the West, he comes by his talent honestly. A frontiersman by heritage (his grandfather was scalped by the Sioux), and a universal man by experience, Louis L'Amour lives the life of his fictional heroes. Since leaving his native Jamestown, North Dakota, at the age of fifteen, he's been a longshoreman, lumberjack, elephant handler, hay shocker, flume builder, fruit picker, and an officer on tank destroyers during World War II. And he's written four hundred short stories and over fifty books (including a volume of poetry).

Mr. L'Amour has lectured widely, traveled the West thoroughly, studied archaeology, compiled biographies of over one thousand Western gunfighters, and read prodigiously (his library holds more than two thousand volumes). And he's watched thirty-one of his westerns as movies. He's circled the world on a freighter, mined in the West, sailed a dhow on the Red Sea, been shipwrecked in the West Indies, stranded in the Mojave Desert. He's won fifty-one of fifty-nine fights as a professional boxer and pinch-hit for Dorothy Kilgallen when she was on vacation from her column. Since 1816, thirty-three members of his family have been writers. And, he says, "I could sit in the middle of Sunset Boulevard and write with my typewriter on my knees; temperamental I am not."

Mr. L'Amour is re-creating an 1865 Western town, christened Shalako, where the borders of Utah, Arizona, New Mexico, and Colorado meet. Historically authentic from whistle to well, it will be a live, operating town, as well as a movie location and tourist attraction.

Mr. L'Amour now lives in Los Angeles with his wife Kathy, who helps with the enormous amount of research he does for his books. Soon, Mr. L'Amour hopes, the children (Beau and Angelique) will be helping too.